Worlds Away From You

By Charlotte Mednick

Charlotte Mednick grew up in Ilfracombe, North Devon in England then went on to receive a First-Class BA (Hons) Multimedia Journalism degree from Solent University in 2017. She continued in education, receiving a Master's Degree in Journalism and Multimedia Communications and now resides in Southampton with her fiancé.

She has always loved YA fiction and enjoyed fiction writing in her spare time, having written fanfiction from a young age then gone on to start creating her own original stories. She's also passionate about musical theater and is a singer, performing with some of Southampton's local musical groups and uploading videos on YouTube since 2014.

She started writing 'Worlds Away From You' whilst studying her MA and it is her first novel.

WORLDS AWAY FROM YOU

Worlds Away From You
(Worlds Away Series, Book One)
By Charlotte Mednick

ISBN 9798670616942
Independently published through
Kindle Direct Publishing
1. Edition, 2020
Papyrus Author, Inc.–Virginia Beach

Book design by Charlotte Mednick
Editing and proofreading by
Julie Hearn and Vicky Soper

http://www.charlottemednick.co.uk
http://www.instagram.com/lottieandherbooks

For Elliot

Chapter 1

RobinM110: *Do you realize we've known each other for three years now?*
MPh2011: *That's crazy... I've never felt closer to someone.*
RobinM110: *Me neither, which is ironic since you live so far away.*
MPh2011: *I wish you could come to London to see me. I want to meet you...*
RobinM1106: *One day...*

"They're here! They're here!" I heard Mom call frantically from downstairs in our lounge. I slammed my laptop shut and ran down to her in a hurry. Mom was kneeling on our sofa, staring out of the window at the front lawn. The house next to ours had been on the market for months and it had become a game between Mom and I to guess who would end up living there.

"How about an exotic Italian stranger who's come to a small town in Colorado to try and find himself?" Mom had suggested as we'd sat one night at our dinner table eating questionable day-old lasagne.

"Okay, two things," I started. "One: Fort Collins isn't a small town, it's a city. Two: I don't think he'll find himself here, most people travel around Europe or Australia or somewhere like that." I remarked with a shrug. Fort Collins definitely wasn't the sort of place you came to find yourself, it was a place to escape from – but I suppose I'm only saying that because I've been stuck here my whole life living in a cul-de-sac.

The cul-de-sac was everything you'd expect from a suburban American neighbourhood. It was tranquil, which was great for studying but boring for growing up as an only child. The trees were lush, and the street was so pristine that you'd think the whole neighbourhood was Photoshopped.

Dad, with a mouthful of food, glanced over at Mom and said, "I don't know how I'd feel if we had a- what was it? 'Exotic Italian stranger' living next door?"

Mom rolled her eyes and I laughed at the two of them. I loved watching my parents together, they were best friends. They always joked with each other, they never argued and if they did, they never held a grudge. That was the kind of love I wanted.

I joined her now, kneeling on the sofa as we stared at the large moving van that was parked outside.

"Alright Robin, last chance to guess." Mom said with anticipation.

"I'm sticking with my Mexican drug cartel idea." I snickered and she shoved me lightly with her elbow. Before we could continue our guessing game, a tall brunette woman climbed out of the van's passenger seat.

"She's pretty." I commented and out of the corner of my eye, I saw Mom nodding her head in agreement, but she never took her eyes off the woman. "Maybe she runs the cartel..." I joked.

"Do you think it's just her?" Mom asked. I shook my head. The house was the same size as ours and every other house on the street. All the houses in the neighbourhood were identical with the exception of the colour or various renovations.

"Not in a house that big," I replied, "I'm betting she has at least two kids." Outside, a man climbed out of the driver's side of the van and both Mom and I raised our eyebrows and our eyes widened.

"Holy shit," Mom mumbled under her breath and I couldn't help but laugh.

"Mom!" I snickered. She laughed and shrugged her shoulders.

"Oh, I'll add a dollar to the jar later" She snickered. "Anyway, can you blame me? Look at him!" She said, gesturing out the window. As she did, the brunette woman glanced up toward us and instinctively we both ducked out of sight of our new neighbours. We laughed with each other and I looked over my shoulder to see Dad standing in the doorway and staring at the two of us.

"Look at who?" He said, before he reached the window and peered out himself. He eyed Mom and I as we continued to hide from the neighbours, shaking his head and munching on a carrot stick.

"Oh, the newbies." He laughed. "It's about time someone moved into that house… though I don't remember seeing these guys visit before."

I looked over the back of the sofa and out the window once more. "Maybe they looked while you were at work." I said. Dad spent a lot of time at his office, but he'd just been made senior partner, so it was to be expected.

An old, dark red car pulled up beside the moving van. It was large; big enough to hold a family and it was covered in scratches and dents. It made me wonder if these people were just reckless drivers or something.

Then I watched as someone else climbed out of the car, someone familiar. A boy around my age with messy brown hair who was tall, with broad shoulders and sunglasses on the top of his head which reflected a ray of sunlight directly into my eye. I squinted and looked away.

"They look nice." Mom said with glee. "And they don't look like a drug cartel of any kind, so I guess we're in the clear."

I looked back out of the window and watched two small children, a toddler and young girl, run toward the front door of their new home. Glancing over, I saw the boy again, lifting a box out of the moving van with ease. He took in his surroundings and as his gaze drifted toward our house, he caught my eye. There was no mistaking – I definitely knew him, and almost immediately my stomach filled with dread. We stared at each other for slightly too long before I hurried out of the room without another word.

Fort Collins may be a small city, but I guess it was slightly too small because I never would have guessed that I'd end up living next to someone I already knew; not just anyone either: Nathaniel Lewis.

Nathaniel was my age; we went to the same school and had some classes together. I don't think we'd ever said a word to one another and I'm certain that he wouldn't know I exist. How could he? I was Robin Montgomery, the shy and quiet girl who never raised her hand in class and never said a word unless she was called on. I stuck with the same two people at school, hung out with the drama club and spent my Friday nights talking to strangers on the internet.

Nathaniel though? He was always the one to make everyone laugh, he came to classes late for no reason and I'm sure his Friday nights were full of parties with more people that wouldn't be caught dead talking to me. Now I had to live next door to him… what kind of fresh hell was this?

Back in my room, I immediately opened my laptop and, as I waited for it to turn on, I looked outside through my bedroom window. I could barely see anything happening at the front of the house. There was a window in the house directly opposite mine – close enough that I could see inside.

I'd enjoyed the last few months of the house being empty. I didn't have to worry about anyone looking into my room; most of all though, it meant I could sit on our side porch roof that lead directly up to my bedroom window. I know I could do that regardless, but I always felt like I was being watched when people lived there, so I'd stopped. Now I'd made the roof a hideaway from the rest of the world. I could sit there and look up at the stars when it wasn't too cloudy, or I could read in the sun when it was warm. I'd lined the roof with string lights and made it a nice haven to go and relax.

I took a seat at my desk and loaded up my internet browser which immediately took me to my favorite website: geeks-haven.com.

I'd found the site when I was twelve. Five years later, I'd found some of my closest friends on that website, but more importantly I'd found love. I know what people say: you can't trust the people you meet online, but I'm an optimist. I've never had reason to believe that anyone I'd met on Geeks Haven wasn't who they said they were.

I met my best friend online: Florence. She's from New York, but we've never met — I feel like our friendship is better for cyberspace. If we met it would be like both of my worlds colliding: my real world and my fantasy world. Online was my fantasy.

Florence had warned me about falling for someone I'd met online one day — 'MPh2011' he called himself. His name was Mason. We met two years after I joined the site, in a chatroom discussing musical theater. He was the sweetest, kindest boy I'd ever met, and he actually noticed me. We clicked instantly. Since then, we'd talked practically every day on the site, and I thought about him all the time. I never thought I'd fall for someone I'd never met, but he made me feel safe. It was like someone had finally accepted me.

As I logged onto the site, I checked who was online. Mason wouldn't be on for a while, he lived in London, and he'd just be starting work. Florence had been active for an hour and a half and it said she was currently in a Harry Potter chatroom.

Clicking on her name, I typed a message:

RobinM110: *The new neighbours have finally arrived.*

Almost instantly I received a response.

TheGreatestFlo: *Mexican drug cartel?*

RobinM110: *Afraid not. It's a nice-looking family... sort of.*

TheGreatestFlo: *Sort of?*

RobinM110: *I know their oldest son. He goes to my school. Let's just say we're at completely different ends of the food chain.*

TheGreatestFlo: *Want me to come beat him up?*

I laughed.

RobinM110: *As much as I'd love to see that, I'm gonna have to say no.*

TheGreatestFlo: *What's his name?*

RobinM110: *Nathaniel…*

A few minutes passed before I received another message from her.

TheGreatestFlo: *He's pretty damn attractive. I'd swipe right on that.*

RobinM110: *…Did you look him up?*

TheGreatestFlo: *You're only friends with one person called Nathaniel on Facebook, you both apparently go to the same school and his profile is public… of course I looked him up.*

RobinM110: *You're so weird.*

TheGreatestFlo: *And you love me for it. Anyway, why are you friends with him on there if you're not really friends?*

RobinM110: *I don't know, isn't everyone friends with everyone on Facebook?*

TheGreatestFlo: *Good point.*

TheGreatestFlo: *Anyway, I have to go, video chat later?*

RobinM110: *Sounds good*

TheGreatestFlo: *Love you Boo*

And, with that she was offline.

I opened my phone and checked what time it was in London. It was 6pm and Mason wouldn't be around for another couple of hours unless he checked his phone during his shift. He worked at a restaurant in the West End and apparently met loads of actors from different shows. It was a dream of mine to see a musical in London with him one day.

I walked over to my bed and sat down on the side, glancing between my phone and my bedroom window. As I looked up, I noticed Nathaniel staring at me through the opposite window and I didn't know what to do.

I looked at him for a few seconds then noticed he was carrying a box labelled 'Nate Bedroom'. He placed it down in the room then walked out without a second glance. Quickly, I shot up and closed the curtain. I sighed deeply, wishfully thinking that the box he carried was labelled wrong.

The last thing I needed was to spend this summer and my senior year with Nathaniel Lewis peeking through my bedroom window and into my life.

Chapter 2

RobinM110: *What's your favorite show you've ever seen?*

MPh2011: *Les Misérables was pretty incredible, but then so was The Book of Mormon.*

RobinM110: *I'm so jealous.*

MPh2011: *We'll see a show together some time. I promise.*

Yawning, I looked at the time on my phone and realised it was nearly 2am. I'd spent the evening talking to Mason and Florence about the new neighbours, but Mason had logged off to go to bed a couple of hours beforehand; he always stayed up late to talk to me. I sent him a quick message to tell him I was going to bed, that I knew he'd see when he woke up.

Looking in the mirror, I noticed that my eyes were slightly red and I realised just how tired I was. I switched off the power for my string lights that lined my window frame and glanced across to the house next door.

The curtains to the opposite window were open and I could see Nathaniel sitting at a desk, writing into a notebook that was barely lit by a desk lamp. He was slouched with his back arched in a chair that looked far too small for him, and he was surrounded by unopened cardboard boxes, all labelled with ‘Nate Bedroom’. He was never called Nate at school, all the teachers and students called him Nathaniel, except his friends who called him Lewis, his surname.

It felt unusual to see him outside of school; it’s like when you’re little and you think your teachers live at school in their classrooms. Obviously, I knew Nathaniel didn’t live at the school, but he was one of those guys that thrives in high school surrounded by people who seemingly adore him and, to someone like me, he essentially didn’t exist outside the threshold of the school gates.

I couldn’t stop staring at him as he sat there. He was wearing an old looking t-shirt with a design I couldn’t make out in the darkness and his usually neatly styled hair looked dishevelled. I couldn't see him that well but when he stood up from his desk, he looked right at me.

He looked confused and that's when I realised the reality of the situation. I was standing at my window in the middle of the night staring into this boy's house on the first night he'd lived there. I pulled the curtains of my window shut quickly and fell back onto my bed, burying my face in my hands. I grabbed my phone, squinting at the screen that shined a little too brightly in my eyes.

Hearing my door creek open, I turned to see my cat Munchkin sauntering into my room, and he jumped up onto my bed and curled up by my feet. Munchkin was a chubby, marmalade Maine Coon cat, impossibly fluffy and the laziest creature I had ever met. Looking through my phone, I felt it buzz and saw a message from Mason.

MPh2011: *Goodnight, sleep well*

I smiled to myself – knowing he must have woken up to send that and taking it as a sign that I should *definitely* go to sleep.

It was only a week into summer vacation, and I was already bored. I'd finished the cheesy romance book I'd saved for the summer within a few days of starting it and there was only so much social media I could scroll through. I slumped down the stairs in my pyjamas with my laptop in hand and headed to the kitchen where I heard my parents chatting and I could smell the familiar scent of breakfast food.

I placed my laptop on the counter and hopped up onto the tall stool with slight difficulty. I was 5'3, so while I wasn't ridiculously small, reaching high shelves and getting comfortable on kitchen stools caused some problems.

I opened my laptop and it flashed on, immediately showing my messages from Florence where I'd left them last night.

"How's the boyfriend?" Mom asked as she spread a slice of toast with peanut butter and gestured to my laptop with the knife. Dad, across the kitchen, rolled his eyes as he continued looking through this morning's mail. He didn't understand my friendships with people I met online and was always questioning if they were real or not.

"I don't like the fact that my daughter could be talking to some 60-year-old creep," I'd heard him say one night in an argument with Mom — one of the few I'd ever heard. Mom had defended my side though, explaining that it wasn't unusual for people my age to be friends with people online. It took some convincing, but he let me keep my social media accounts as long as I agreed to never meet up with anyone I'd met online, and if I was absolutely desperate then either he or Mom would have to be present. It was a sacrifice I'd been more than willing to make… that is, before I fell for Mason, and before the longing to finally meet him had caught up with me. These days all I wanted was to hop on a plane and be by his side, but I'm pretty sure that would push Dad over the edge.

"He's okay." I replied, unable to stop a small smile from creeping onto my lips. "He's going to see a show tonight." I added, watching Mom place the uncut slice of toast between her teeth and letting it hang out of her mouth. She wiped her hands on a dish towel and walked over to Dad to fix his tie and collar.

"Another one?" Dad replied. "Where does he get the money to go to all these shows?" He asked as he watched Mom get some rogue crumbs on the collar of his freshly washed shirt, but I could tell he was only half-interested in Mason… probably not even half.

"He has a job, I told you that." I didn't like talking to Dad about Mason. No matter how hard I tried to make him understand, he would never be fully on-board, and I knew that, but he didn't realize that Mason was just as important to me as he or Mom were. Mason has been there while I've grown up, I've opened up to him, and he's done the same to me. More importantly, we get each other.

None of my friends, not even Florence, understand my love for the theater. Mom took me to see Hairspray when I was younger, and it changed my life. The music, the lights and the atmosphere, the fact that it was all live and happening before my very eyes. When I found Mason, and he understood that feeling, something clicked. He's made me feel comfortable talking about that passion, and I love him for it.

"Of course." Dad replied, putting the mail he was looking at down on the counter and taking a glance at his watch. "I better head off." He said, kissing Mom on the forehead.

"Oh, come on, give me a real kiss." Mom said, placing the now half-eaten toast down onto a plate.

"Not after you've eaten peanut butter, your breath stinks." He said, holding his hand up and covering my mom's mouth. I laughed as I watched Mom mumble incoherently into his hand. He moved his hand as Mom leaned in for a kiss, causing Dad to shake his head at her as he held his breath jokingly.

"Fine." Mom said, backing down then suddenly blew a big peanut-scented breath into his face, causing both me and her to laugh as Dad sauntered out of the room. "You owe me a kiss!" she called to him.

"Only after you brush your teeth!" I heard him shout back and then listened as he left the house, forcefully pulling the front door closed. The door had been stiff and broken for as long as I could remember.

"So, Robin, have you found yourself a job yet?" Mom asked as she sat down on the stool beside me to finish eating her breakfast.

She'd spent the last couple of months persuading me to get a job and start saving money for college next year, and it's not like I hadn't tried to find one, but nothing seemed to work out for me. Now that it was summer, and I was constantly home, she was more adamant than ever.

"Nope..." I said casually, hoping she'd drop the subject… she didn't.

"Honey, you only have a year left of high school before you're off living your life and I want to make sure you're-"

"Prepared." I said, cutting her off to finish the sentence I'd heard a million times. "Is there even any point me getting a job? I need to spend the summer preparing for senior year, and I can't even commit to a full-time job since I'm going to have to quit at the end of the summer anyway."

"You could work weekends while you're at school," she responded quickly, as if the idea had been in her head this whole time. "Just because your father and I are helping pay your tuition doesn't mean we're going to be there whenever you need money."

"I know." I said, barely listening as I stared at my laptop screen as Mason's name popped up with a message. I couldn't help but smile. I opened it.

***MPh2011:** I'm bored, you busy?*

***RobinM110:** Just listening to my mom give me the "you need a job!" speech... the usual.*

***MPh2011:** that sucks.*

***RobinM110:** Tell me about it.*

***MPh2011:** wish I could be there with you... I could give you a cuddle.*

***RobinM110:** I wish you could be too.*

I could feel the butterflies in my stomach and the heat in my cheeks. Something about Mason was so wonderful, how he made me feel so loved without even being here. As I went to type another message, I saw Mom glaring at me from the other side of the kitchen — I hadn't even notice her stand up and walk over there.

I shut my laptop, looking guilty. Mom supported my decision to be with Mason — even if she didn't quite understand it, but there was a limit, and she was still my mom.

"Chat to your boyfriend later," she said, exasperated. "We're going next door to meet the neighbours… see what their deal is."

"What do you mean 'we'?" I asked, although I already knew the answer.

Chapter 3

MPh2011: *Have you thought any more about my suggestion?*

RobinM110: *I'm still not sure, I am considering it though, I promise*

There was nothing I wanted to do less today than go and act neighbourly with the newbies, especially knowing that I would have to be polite and civil to a boy who could not be further away from me on the school hierarchy. It's not that I wasn't polite, don't get me wrong — I'd done the whole "welcome to the neighbourhood" thing with new people, but normally they're total strangers, and we often never talk to them again (except for the occasional pleasantries at the grocery store or something).

Nathaniel wasn't a stranger though, he was a boy who spent an entire year in middle school throwing balls of paper at me and my friends in math class; the boy who laughed with his friends and made crude jokes during sex ed and the boy who now wouldn't even look in my direction at school on the off chance he'd lose some of his 'cool rep' or whatever.

Mom packed some shop-bought brownies in a Tupperware box as I got changed into something more appropriate than my pyjamas. I settled on a red and white striped oversized t-shirt and a pair of slightly ripped shorts with my favorite sneakers. I'd had them since freshman year, the laces were entirely frayed, and I can't remember a day where I didn't wear them unless I was forced to go to a formal event of some sort.

I strolled down the stairs and walked into the kitchen to see Mom putting the now empty brownie packaging into the trash. "Packing them in a box doesn't make them homemade. That's cheating." I said, raising my eyebrow.

"It's only cheating if they find out." Mom responded and I snickered.

"I'll remember that when I take my SATs this fall." I responded with a grin.

"Don't you dare." She said, grabbing the Tupperware box and her keys from the counter. I looked her up and down and noticed her now curled hair and fresh makeup. my mom was one of my favorite people; she was funny, hard-working, and I was jealous of how pretty she was, even in her forties. I never looked in the mirror and thought of myself like I thought of her, I just kind of… dealt with my looks — my too-long blonde hair, my short legs and tiny stature. I just felt so small. I hated feeling small.

As we walked across the lawn, I stared at their house for what felt like the millionth time — except this time it wasn't totally empty. Through the windows I could see stacks of boxes and plastic wrapped furniture. It was like it was lived in but not quite a home. I put my hands in my pockets awkwardly as we stepped onto their porch and I watched Mom knock on the door. She nudged me with her elbow, and I looked up at her. "Please try and look happy."

The tall man we saw by the moving van yesterday answered the door. "Can I help you?" He asked. His face was sweaty, and he stroked his overgrown patchy gray beard. He looked exactly like Nathaniel, just older. He had wrinkles on his forehead and bags under his eyes and a general look of tiredness.

"Yes, yes, I'm Amanda, this is my daughter Robin." Mom said with a smile, holding out her hand for a handshake while tucking the box of definitely-homemade-and-not-store-bought brownies under her other arm. "We live next door," she added.

"Oh hi!" He said, his demeanour changing almost instantly. A smile leapt onto his face as he took mom's hand in his. "Nice to meet you. Do you want to come in?"

"We'd love to." Mom replied, and she pulled me into the house, following the man. I just wanted to go back to my room and read a book or talk to Mason, but I suppose there'd be no way to get out of this without looking rude.

"I'm Geoff." He said, walking us through the house toward the kitchen. "My wife is Caitlyn, she's upstairs with the kids." He said. "She'd love to meet you."

"Lovely." Mom said, "My husband is Kyle but he's at work. We brought you some brownies, you know… as a welcome to the neighbourhood kind of thing." She said, holding out the box.

"Oh great, thank you." He said politely, taking the box from my mother and placing it on their kitchen counter. I looked around their kitchen and noticed an unopened box of the same brownies Mom had played off as her own. I couldn't help but snicker quietly to myself. It was weird being in this house. It was practically identical to my own, except the walls were a disgusting pale mustard colour with patches of wet and fresh pastel purple paint which looked a lot nicer. There was a tub of paint resting on a step stool near the kitchen and it made the whole house smell like chemical fumes.

"So, what made you move to our little city?" Mom asked with a smile.

"Oh, we've lived in Fort Collins for years, we just… needed a change of scenery I guess." He said, but the whole atmosphere in the room changed. Something shifted when he said it, but I couldn't put my finger on what and why. Maybe he was just tired. "We probably would have moved away but my son's just going into his senior year so we thought it would be best to keep him in the same school."

"Oh really?" Mom said and her voice perked up. "Robin's starting senior year too!" She said, patting me on the back, and they both looked at me. I think they expected me to say something.

"Um… yeah." I said, awkwardly, mentally slapping myself for being so socially inept.

"Do you know my son, Nathaniel?" He asked and I stuffed my hands back in my pockets. "Nathaniel Lewis."

"Sure." I answered. "Sort of. We're not really friends but I know of him." I added.

"Did I hear my name?" Someone said from behind us and I turned around to see Nathaniel walking in with a cardboard box in his arms. It looked heavy and his arms were tensed, showing off his biceps in a tight black t-shirt. I gulped nervously. "I think this got mixed up with my bedroom stuff." He said, placing the box which was labelled 'kitchen' beside me on the counter.

"Yes, you heard correctly." Geoff said. "This is Amanda and Robin; they live next door." He said, gesturing to us.

Immediately I felt a knot tighten in my stomach and my instincts were telling me to run and get out of this house. I didn't belong in the same vicinity as Nathaniel Lewis, let alone in his house and partaking in a friendly conversation with him.

"I know," He replied with a shrug. "You were staring into my bedroom window last night."

My eyes widened at his bluntness and I felt the blush rush to my cheeks. What a great first(ish) impression. "Although… do I know you?" He asked, raising an eyebrow at me, and grabbing a brownie from the box, taking a bite. I didn't say anything, I just nodded.

"You go to school together." Geoff replied, and I was secretly thankful that he had so that I didn't have to speak. I felt my phone vibrate in my pocket and pulled it out discreetly, it was Mason.

MPh2011: *How's it going?*

I smiled a little and it helped me relax. Mom and Geoff had now moved onto a conversation about the neighbourhood; how small it was, how it was a nice area where nothing interesting happened. Nathaniel started opening the box he'd brought in and unpacking an assortment of pots and pans into an empty cupboard. I looked back down at my phone and replied to Mason.

RobinM110: *If a hole could open up right now in the floor and suck me into another dimension that would be stupendous*

MPh2011: *That bad?*

RobinM110: *That bad.*

"What're you grinning at?" Nathaniel asked and I looked up at him. He was staring at my phone and drinking a can of soda.

"Nothing." I answered quickly, sliding the phone back into my pocket.

"Sure..." He rolled his eyes, turning his attention back to the box on the counter and continuing to unpack it.

"You know, I think Nate's restaurant is hiring." I heard Geoff say and both Nathaniel and I turned our heads toward our parents.

"Oh really?" Mom said enthusiastically. "Robin, did you hear that?" She said, tapping me slightly too hard on the arm to get my attention, even though she already had it.

"Yeah, I heard." I said and I couldn't help but glance at Nathaniel, who was looking back at me now.

Geoff had a small smile on his face and looked to his son. "Didn't you say something on the phone to your friend about The Kingfisher hiring waiting staff?"

"Well, I mean, yeah but-" Nathaniel started but his Dad cut him off.

"Great! Then you can put in a good word for Robin and that's everyone's problems sorted." He smiled and Mom looked thrilled. It was almost like she was excited at the idea of getting me out of the house for the summer.

"Geoff!" I heard a yell from upstairs and he sighed softly.

"And that would be Caitlyn." He said. "I'll bring her down and introduce her."

We spent the next hour with Nathaniel's parents eating the definitely-homemade-and-not-store-bought brownies. Our moms seemed to get on well, Mom suggested a book for Caitlyn to read when she had a spare moment, to which she'd agreed but admitted that she wouldn't have much time between unpacking and looking after her younger children. I met them briefly when they ran downstairs to find Nathaniel.

A young girl, probably about eight or nine who had a short bob haircut and lots of freckles, much like her Mom, and a young boy who couldn't have been more than three who had run into the kitchen butt-naked. Nathaniel had taken them both upstairs and left Mom and me with his parents. It was weirdly comfortable being around them, they seemed like nice people and not nearly as intimidating as their son — I suppose cliques at high school had that effect.

When we finally left, we said goodbye to Geoff and Caitlyn and Mom gave them both a hug. "They were great." She said as we walked back across the lawns. "And you might have a job too!" She clapped her hands together, excitedly.

"Great…" I mumbled, not nearly as enthusiastically.

Chapter 4

RobinM110: *I think I've made a decision...*

MPh2011: *Oh?*

RobinM110: *I'll look into it.*

Ever since my freshman year I'd been researching colleges. I know some people have their colleges picked out since kindergarten, but I'd been trying to convince Dad to let me go to acting school since I was in middle school, and he'd never been entirely on board. He always suggested joining an amateur theater group and studying "a more academic major".

My dad's a lawyer and had been pushed into that career by his own parents, but he was always very clever, and he loved his job regardless of whether it was his choice or not. I'm not very academic and performing is what I always loved to do. Mom put me in ballet classes when I was five and a youth theater project on the side – since then I never stopped.

I'd spent the last couple of months talking to people on Geeks Haven about what colleges were best, I spoke to Mason about what he thought I should do and I decided his idea wasn't all that bad. I'd been sceptical, but I think it could be good.

As I sat at the dinner table with my parents, I pushed a couple of meatballs around my plate, trying to pluck up the courage to tell them mine and Mason's plans.

Mom and Dad had spent the day helping Geoff and Caitlyn unpack while I'd looked at colleges. This is the first time I'd seen my parents make such an effort with new people in the neighbourhood.

I think Mom liked the idea of making more friends since she spent most of her time either at work at a convenience store or in her art studio painting canvases for her online store. That's why she was always encouraging my creativity, she was the same.

"So… I've decided on some of the colleges I want to apply for." I started. No turning back now. My parents attention turned to me, both clearly looking optimistic.

"Mmhmm?" Dad mumbled with a mouth full of spaghetti. I took a deep breath knowing he wasn't going to be happy with my choices.

"Julliard, Carnegie Mellon, Columbia, AMDA and The Royal Academy of Dramatic Art in London." I said quickly and stuffed my fork full of spaghetti in my mouth. Dad didn't look pleased, neither did Mom when I said the last school.

Mason had been trying to convince me to come and study in London for the last few months. I never thought it could even be a possibility, but to make him happy I decided to research it — what was the harm? If I did end up going to London I'd finally be with Mason and studying something I love. Mason was happy when I'd told him I'd look into it, the idea that I could be moving away from home and to him seemed to make him as excited as I was, Secretly, I wished I was already there. As much as I loved my parents, I loved Mason too and I wanted to be with him now.

"Did you say London?" Mom asked, and I could tell by her tone that she was upset at the news.

"Mason suggested I have a look at performing arts schools there and it looked really good and-" I started, trying to defend my decision before Dad cut me off.

"So, this is about that boy?" He asked, putting his fork down and staring at me.

"Well… no. It's about me and what I want to do but if I can be with Mason too then it's a win-win." I defended.

"I think this boy is clouding your judgement, Robin." Dad said, shaking his head. "You've never met the kid and yet you're willing to move across the world for this fantasy."

"Fantasy?" I asked, raising my voice a little, upset.

"Yes! You don't know who this person is, you can't pick up your whole life to go and live with them!" His voice was also beginning to get louder.

"I do know him!" I argued, slamming my fork down on the table. I was at my limit with my dad's criticism.

"It's bad enough that you're going to be spending the money your mother and I have been saving for your whole life on some impractical dream of dancing around on a stage! I'm not going to indulge more of your nonsense!"

"Kyle…" Mom said quietly, reaching over and grabbing my dad's hand. I stood up angrily, forcefully shoving my chair backward causing it to topple onto the floor.

"Just because I don't want to be some snotty lawyer doesn't mean that my dreams are impractical! And at least Mason has faith in me, that's more than I can say for you!" I yelled and stormed off upstairs to my room. I heard Dad call my name, but I didn't go back. I slammed my bedroom door and sat on the edge of my bed, wiping the tears from my eyes.

I hated arguing with my parents, especially because it didn't happen often, and I knew that by this time tomorrow it would have blown over and I'd probably end up sitting down with Dad and having a conversation about it all. It's what we always did. We'd sit with each other, watch a movie, and listen to each other's points of view. It was something Mom came up with when my parents started dating, and they'd get into their rare fights, a way to understand the other side but in a comfortable and prepared situation rather than spontaneously. I think it's why I didn't see them argue now. Mom was a fixer, and with Dad and I it did help.

I glanced out my window, wiping my eyes again and investigated Nathaniel's room. It was empty–maybe he was at work at The Kingfisher. I grabbed my phone and headphones and climbed out of the window to sit on the porch roof. I clicked the switch for the string lights, and they lit up the roof dimly. I opened the musical theater playlist on my phone and sat with my knees pressed into my chest. To one side of me, I could see the town, lit up like a Christmas tree in the slowly dimming evening and behind all the houses to the other side, the distant mountains towered over the city's outlying hills and trees. What I wouldn't give to be out of this city and on the other side of them.

I sighed and noticed a few messages from Florence and Mason on my phone. I didn't want to talk to anyone right now. I loved them both so much, but they weren't here, and no matter how much faith they had in me about going to college and achieving whatever dreams I had, it didn't make a difference to my current situation. I loved them for their unwavering support — I had the most amazing friend and boyfriend ever but sometimes though, I just had to be alone. I laid back on the roof, admiring the oranges, blues and purples that were painted across the evening sky before closing my eyes and listening to my music, blocking out the rest of the world.

After a few songs played, I felt something tapping against my foot and I shot up, startled, to see Nathaniel leaning out his window and poking me. "Fucking hell!" I exclaimed without thinking and I pulled my headphones off. Nathaniel just laughed.

"I did try to get your attention, but your music was too loud, I could hear it from here." He said, moving slightly back into his room but staying close to the window. "What're you doing out there?"

"Nothing…" I said, immediately feeling awkward again. I felt like a deer in headlights whenever Nathaniel talked to me; like every human interaction I'd ever had was erased from my memory and I had no knowledge of how to talk to another person. I just panicked.

“Well that’s not true.” He commented, gesturing to my headphones and phone laying on the roof. “What were you listening to?” He asked.

I don’t know why he cared or why he was even talking to me, but I sighed and indulged him. “The Last Five Years...” I responded truthfully.

“The what?” He asked. I rolled my eyes as he said, “Is that some sort of indie band?”

“No, it’s a musical.” I said bluntly.

“Oh… weird.” He said and I raised my eyebrow.

“Why is that weird?” I asked, fully prepared for an obnoxious comeback.

“Oh, I guess it’s not. I don’t know.” He said and an awkward silence fell in the air between us. “Wait! I know you now, you were in the school talent show last year, weren’t you?”

This took me a little by surprise, not only because it was almost a year ago but because I performed with the school glee club and only had a one line solo. “Yeah…”

“I knew I recognised you.” He said, as if knowing me was some big achievement.

“You know we’re in the same History class right, and Math... and English?” I said, bursting his bubble.

I could tell I’d made this whole conversation a lot more awkward. “Um…” Nathaniel mumbled, looking anywhere but at me.

“Good to know I make an impact.” I said before I could stop myself. We both waited in silence, hoping the other person would say something.

He reached his arm up and rubbed the back of his neck, biting his bottom lip and looking guilty. I couldn’t help but admire his good looks. The way his arm tensed and the way his hair fell so gracefully yet effortlessly down to his eyes. It was easy to understand why so many girls in school liked him. I shook the thoughts from my head as he started speaking again. “They’re not my strongest subjects.” He said.

“Well, football’s not my strongest subject but I know you’re the quarterback.” I replied which made him chuckle.

"Everyone knows I'm the quarterback." He snickered and I just rolled my eyes and stared at him. The way he acted was ridiculous, it seemed like he was trying purposely to be obnoxious.

"Is that supposed to impress me?" I asked, not bothering to beat around the bush anymore. If Nathaniel Lewis was going to be living next door acting this stuck up, then what was the point in being shy? I might as well give him a taste of his own medicine. Plus, I didn't have the energy after the night I'd had to even think before I spoke.

He looked me up and down and all the confidence I had melted away. It felt like he was dissecting me with his eyes, so I folded my arms in front of my stomach, tapping my foot anxiously. "It impresses most people." He eventually said.

I looked him up and down like he did with me. Before I could even think about it, I said "sorry to be the bearer of bad news but the whole 'high school poster boy' thing doesn't really impress me that much." and even I was surprised at my words. I stared at the boy in front of me, feeling tense, and suddenly became very aware that almost every girl in my school would kill to be in my position right now. I saw him smirk, and I relaxed a little. Beside me my phone vibrated, and I looked down to see a message from Mason.

MPh2011: *I can't sleep and you're not replying… is everything okay?*

I couldn't help but smile a little. He was concerned and it made me feel loved.

"Anyone interesting?" Nathaniel asked and I looked back up at him. He was staring at my phone in my hand. I shrugged.

"My boyfriend." I told him and he looked surprised. "What?" I asked as he folded his arms across his chest, staring right at me.

"You just don't seem like the type." He commented and when he saw my clearly offended expression he continued "I mean like… you just seem… I don't know."

"Well… thank you for that eye-opening explanation, Nathaniel Lewis, you've changed my life." I told him, turning around, and opening my window to head back inside. “I’ll see you around.” I said sarcastically, with no intention of that happening.

“I hope so.” He said and I felt my cheeks flush.

I climbed back into my bedroom and laid on my bed. I felt a pit in my stomach and remembered my fight with Dad. While I was out on the roof, it was like it hadn’t even happened, but crossing the threshold into the house brought it all flooding back. I just wish he’d understand me. I’m sure if Mom ended up being across the world, he wouldn’t think twice about going to be with her and I don’t understand why chasing my dream of performing was such a bad thing in his eyes. I sighed and messaged Mason back.

RobinM110: *Had a fight with Dad. It’ll cool off by tomorrow but I’m going to have an early night. Get some sleep, I’ll talk to you tomorrow.*

Almost instantly I received a response.

MPh2011: *I love you*

I smiled down at my phone screen, feeling my heart flutter slightly in my chest.

RobinM110: *I love you too*

Chapter 5

RobinM110: *So, my dad doesn't want me coming to London.*

MPh2011: *Well it's not his decision, just ignore him.*

RobinM110: *He's still my dad, I need to listen.*

"Ready guys?" My dance teacher, Miss Madison, asked my class as we sat on the studio floor having a quick break. I loved Miss Madison so much, she was as passionate about dance as I was, and more importantly she understood my love of musical theater. Every couple of months we learnt a routine to a song from a musical — she kept it limited so the dancers who weren't as interested didn't get bored. This time we'd learnt a dance to a Taylor Swift song, I hadn't heard it before this week which was apparently a crime based on how some of the other dancers reacted when I told them. Miss Madison must have been in her mid-twenties, and she studied at The New York

Performing Arts Academy, she was exactly what I wanted to be… except I wanted to be on-stage, not teaching a group of teenagers. I always wondered why she'd chosen this instead.

I took a final gulp of my water and stood up, holding out my hand and helping my friend Kelly up from the floor.

"Let's do this!" She said, and we put our water bottles on the floor next to the wall at the edge of the room. She was always so enthusiastic… almost sickeningly so. I pushed my hair back out of my face, wiping some of the sweat from my forehead. We'd been in class for nearly two hours now and this was the last run through of the routine for the day.

We got into our positions and I stared at myself in the large mirror in front of me. Miss Madison started the music, and we began the routine, twisting and turning and moving to the beat. I performed my moves with the other girls and boys in the group. I glanced back at myself in the mirror as I turned into my next move and caught sight of someone in the reflection by the studio door. As I kept moving to the music, I glanced to the side and saw Nathaniel standing by the door. Shocked, I missed the next couple of beats of the song and bumped into Jason, one of three boys in my class. He carried on the dance as if nothing happened and I followed his lead, getting back into the flow of the routine. Although, I couldn't stop myself from glancing in the reflection when I got a chance and looking in Nathaniel's direction. Why was he here?

"Concentrate Robin!" Miss Madison called over the music and I put my focus back into the routine, moving my body with the sound. When the dance finished, I could feel myself breathing heavily and we all took a moment to collect ourselves. Everyone separated and grabbed their things, and I quickly grabbed my water bottle and made my way to Nathaniel.

"Can I help you?" I said, taking a swig from my water. Nathaniel was looking me up and down — something he seemed to do a lot. I suddenly felt very exposed in my dance wear, a pair of tight black activewear leggings and a gray crop top. Not something I'd wear regularly. I pushed my hair out of my face as he stared at me. I coughed purposefully to get his attention.

“Nice dance.” He commented and I felt the sides of my mouth twitch into a small smile. No one normally watched us, but that didn’t take away from the fact that the school’s quarterback seemed to be stalking me.

“Thanks… why are you here exactly?” I asked, trying to prompt a proper response from him this time.

“Your Mom told me to find you here.” He said, but that didn’t make the situation any clearer or less weird.

“Okay…” I said and there was a long silence hanging in the air where we just looked at each other. He was quite a bit taller than me, maybe just less than a foot, so I stared up at him. His hair was pushed back, and it looked fluffy and freshly washed. I hadn’t noticed originally, but he’d stepped a little closer to me and I felt my breathing hitch in my throat. Being this close, I could smell his deodorant, and it made me acutely aware that he could probably smell my sweat. Snapping myself away from these thoughts, I said “That doesn’t explain why you’re here…”

I felt someone pat me on the shoulder and turned to see Kelly. She pulled me into a quick and slightly sweaty hug. “See you next week, yeah?” She said and I hugged her back, nodding. “He’s cute.” She whispered in my ear before turning and heading out of the door and I chuckled a little. The class filed out and Miss Madison walked over to us.

“And you are?” She asked, eyeing up Nathaniel.

“Nate.” He said, holding out his hand as a formality, much like his father had when I’d first met him. I wondered if he preferred being called Nate. Everyone at school always called him Nathaniel, so I just followed suit.

“You’re a very fit young lad,” Miss Madison started and I shuffled away to grab my bag, leaving them to it but as the dance studio was now empty I could still hear everything.

“Thinking of joining the class?” She asked and I scoffed. They both turned to me and I looked away, embarrassed.

“Oh God, no.” He responded. “I’m a football player not a… ballerina.” I shook my head at this comment as I packed my bag with my bottle and sweatshirt. It was too hot outside, especially after that workout, to even think about wearing it. “Just came to pick up Robin is all.” He said and my ears perked up. Picking me up? What?

“This isn’t ballet,” Miss Madison replied, and I walked over to the two of them, swinging my bag over my shoulder. “Ballerina’s are swans. My class are sexy lions and lionesses.” She told him and as she said it, he looked down at me.

“You can say that again.” He smirked and I felt my cheeks heat up. Instinctively, I pulled on the hem of my crop top, trying to cover myself up a little and questioned my decision not to wear my sweatshirt after all.

“Jesus Christ.” I muttered under my breath. “Sorry about him. I’ll see you next week.” I told her, and she patted me on the shoulder, and I moved past Nathaniel and headed outside.

I heard footsteps behind me and sighed. Nathaniel jogged a little to catch up with me and walked beside me. I held my bag straps tight, twiddling my thumbs as we walked. “Why are you here again?” I asked. “My mom’s supposed to take me home, I'm having a movie night with my dad."

"Well you'll just have to reschedule that because your Mom has sent me here to get you and take you toooooo..." He said, putting his hand on my bare lower back and I shuddered a little at his touch. He guided me over to his beat-up little car and unlocked the doors, opening the passenger side door and leaning in to find something.

"To…?" I prompted, watching him, and trying to get a glimpse of what he was doing.

"Little lady's got no patience." He mocked, grabbing something from the car and hiding it behind his back. I crossed my arms over my chest and tapped my foot impatiently. "Drumroll please…" He said, looking at me expectantly but I just stood there looking at him. "I'm not telling you anything else until you do a drumroll."

I rolled my eyes. "I'm not doing a drumroll." I told him plainly. "You're practically a stranger and you expect me to get into your car for you to take me to some mysterious location? No thanks."

"It wouldn't be a mystery if you'd just do a drumroll." He said, leaning back against the car and staring at me. We just stood there staring at each other but after a while I resigned to the fact that he was too stubborn to just tell me what was going on.

"Fine!" I said, defeated. I tapped a barely enthusiastic drumroll on my thighs and watched him as he pulled a balled-up navy blue t-shirt out from behind his back and threw it at me. I caught it and looked down at it. "Your first shift as a waitress at the Kingfisher restaurant." He told me and my mouth fell open and eyes went wide.

"My what as a *what*?" I asked, annoyed. Had he planned this with my mom? "What the fuck are you talking about?"

"Language little lady!" He sneered and I threw the t-shirt at him, frustrated.

"Stop calling me that!" I moaned, and he tossed the t-shirt back in my direction.

"Look, your Mom was at my house hanging out with my parents and asked me to do you a favor so I'm doing it. Trust me, I wanted to get this job for my friend Shaun, but

Mom insisted I give you a go. I'm only doing it for her, so would you just get in the car and come to the restaurant because our shift starts in about 30 minutes." He explained and I was a little taken aback. I knew Mom had spent a lot of time at his house with his parents since they'd moved in last week, she'd made good friends with them, but why hadn't she said anything to me about this arrangement?

I unfolded the t-shirt in my hand and saw that it had his name written messily inside the collar with a black marker. "This is yours?" I asked, giving up the fight and walking toward the car. Maybe doing a shift at the restaurant wouldn't be so bad… and it might help ease the situation with Dad. Nathaniel walked around to the driver's seat and climbed in and I followed suit, sitting in the passenger seat and looking around. There were children's toys and a dusting of crumbs in the back seat and fast food containers on the floor — definitely a family car.

"You don't work at the restaurant officially, so you don't have a uniform. You can borrow that for now." He said, flipping his hair out of his face and starting the car, checking the rear mirror, and reversing out of the parking space.

I placed my bag down in between my feet and held the t-shirt on my lap. Normally in a situation like this I'd grab my phone and message Florence, but I never take it to dance class so that I don't get distracted. I would have brought it if I'd known I wouldn't be going straight home.

"It's huge." I said, glancing at the label with the letter 'L' sewn in. Normally with unisex clothes I was an XS, this would look like a dress on me.

"How rude." He snickered, and I knew he was joking. "Tuck it in." He shrugged, keeping his eyes on the road. I shook my head at his suggestion.

"Into my leggings?" I asked, rhetorically. Instead, I pulled it over my head, covering my crop top and stomach, awkwardly manoeuvring it around my seatbelt. I took it in my hands and tied it in a tight knot at my hips. I felt a bit more comfortable now I wasn't wearing something as exposing as my dance gear, but the t-shirt had a strong scent of Nathaniel.

I pulled my hair out from the collar of the t-shirt and let it flow down my back then glanced over at him in the driver's seat. He was looking at me out of the corner of his eye, but he quickly turned his attention back to the road.

"Do you prefer Nate or Nathaniel? Because I swear, I've never heard anyone at school call you Nate." I asked in a sad attempt to make conversation.

"Only the people who don't really know me call me Nathaniel. I prefer Nate though." He said. "You can call me Nate." He added and a small smile crept onto my lips.

Suddenly, the thought of Mason in London just finishing work entered my head and I felt guilty, like I'd done something wrong, but I couldn't figure out what. Maybe being in the same vicinity as a guy like Nate had that effect, but I pushed the thoughts away. It's not like I'd planned this, it's not my fault.

"Okay… Nate it is." I said, looking out at the road. We spent the next few minutes not speaking and listening to the radio. A few songs played before Nate finally spoke up.

"So… you dance." He said and I glanced back over to him.

"What a keen observation." I commented and he laughed. I liked his smile; it was slightly crooked, and I found myself thinking that was probably his only physical imperfection. Even with that though, it seemed to make him more attractive.

"It… looked cool" He said, and I couldn't help but let out a small laugh. "How long have you been doing that?"

"You don't have to pretend to care, just so you know." I told him honestly, and he glanced over at me again before turning back to the road.

"I'm not pretending, you looked hot, I'm surprised you're not a cheerleader." He said and I scoffed. A cheerleader? No thanks. That whole group of girls were some of the most stuck up, self-absorbed people I'd ever met. I don't want to sound snobby; I can appreciate the art of cheering but being part of the cheer squad was the last thing I wanted to do.

"Not really the same thing." I said simply. I brushed past the fact that he called me hot, mainly because there was literally no part of my being that knew how to respond to that comment, especially from a person who's not my boyfriend, and even more so when that person is Nate.

"Anyway…" I started, wanting to move the conversation along. "What am I actually going to be doing tonight? And how long am I here for?" Nate was tapping the steering wheel with his index finger along to the beat of whatever song was playing on the radio, pulling into a line of traffic.

"Waitressing. You'll take people's orders, put the order through and take them their food. It's only four hours tonight, and you'll be paid too." He explained and I listened carefully. "I work in the kitchen, so I won't really be around, but if you need a hand with anything, you'll be with a waiter called Danny. I don't know him that well, but he'll be able to help." He said and I immediately felt nervous, twiddling my thumbs. "Literally all it is is picking up plates and taking them to different parts of the restaurant." He said, as if it was the easiest thing ever.

I sat there silently and looked out at the road. I could see The Kingfisher in the distance and immediately felt sick to my stomach. I hadn't even had a chance to shower or make myself presentable after my class. Quickly, I pulled down the sun visor in front of me in the hopes there would be a mirror on the inside and a photograph fell out of it and onto my lap. I picked it up and looked down, for the brief moment I looked at it, I saw it was a family photo. Nate was on the side next to his Dad with a huge smile on his face but before I could take a real look, Nate snatched it out of my hand.

"Didn't realize that was there, sorry." He said, pulling into a parking space in the staff parking lot and tucking the photograph into the pocket of his jeans. I shrugged it off and checked my reflection in the sun visor mirror, fixing my hair and taking a deep breath. Nate parked the car and looked over at me.

"Ready?" He asked.

"Nope." I answered instinctively, "I was ready to go home and watch a movie with my dad and take a shower because I smell like death after that class. I was not ready to spend four hours without my phone waiting on tables in my dance leggings and stinking of sweat."

"It's really not that bad." He reassured me as he opened the car door and climbed out. "And honestly if you hate it that much you can leave or just… escape to the kitchen and help me wash dishes." He said. The thought of that did make me feel slightly better about it. Not that I thought of us as friends at all, but if Nate is the only person in the whole place, I know then I suppose spending four hours with him wouldn't be the worst thing in the world.

"Order for Table 17!" I heard a chef call out from the kitchen. I was currently hiding in a storage cupboard in the hallway between the restaurant bar and the kitchen. I told Danny, the waiter who was training me, I was going to the bathroom and I'd now been in the cupboard for about fifteen minutes, and I'm sure Danny would be questioning my health. Nate had forgotten to mention that children could eat free every Thursday at The Kingfisher, so it was one of the busiest nights of the week, with screaming and crying children all over the place. This (as well as creepy old men at the bar eating plates of shrimp and drinking away their troubles, and a bachelorette party) meant that this had ended up being one of the busiest nights of the year. I'd already dropped five glasses of soda by falling over a baby's highchair and smashed them all over the floor, taken the wrong order to multiple tables and got yelled at by one customer for messing up. Danny had explained to the man that it was my first day, but they'd complained so much that they were given their meals for free.

Peering out of a crack in the door, I looked at a clock on the wall and realised I'd been here for three and a half hours now. Taking a deep breath, I walked back to the kitchen to find Nate bobbing along to the radio that was playing quietly in the background. I bit my lip lightly and smiled, walking over to him, and standing awkwardly beside a counter stacked with freshly cleaned plates. A waitress who'd spent the whole evening coming into the kitchen to talk to Nate leaned around me and grabbed one from the pile, glaring at me.

"You alright there, little lady?" Nate said, still bobbing along to the music.

"Please stop calling me that." I told him, rolling my eyes. "I can't be out there anymore. I've already spent a whole fifteen minutes in the storage cupboard hiding from Danny and I'm pretty sure I made a child cry earlier by just handing her a box of crayons, which makes no sense." I explained and Nate laughed, shaking his head.

"Kids cry, that's not your fault." He said. I looked at him washing the dishes. I always thought of him as an obnoxious jock but since he came into my life, he'd changed that opinion… at least slightly. He seemed caring enough, definitely not completely unbearable like I'd pictured — but could I see us actually being friends? No.

I spent my time at school with two people from the drama and glee club and ate lunch in the auditorium. Nate ate his lunch in the cafeteria at the 'cool table' with about 20 different people and more often than not with a different girl hanging off of his arm. The thought of being back at school brought back the whole argument I had with Dad. I wanted to study performing arts and if I could go to London and be with Mason then that would be a dream… I just had to convince him.

"I don't handle pressure very well… and being a waitress is a lot of pressure." I told him, shuffling my feet awkwardly. "Plus, I'm so tired from dance class and if I had to come here after class every time then I'd be so drained every night." I explained, trying to come up with various excuses not to come back. Nate grabbed a dish towel and handed it over.

"If you're going to stand here, you can help out." He told me and handed me a freshly washed glass, brushing my hand with his soap-covered rubber gloves. I could see him peering at me through the corner of his eye. "So, how long have you been dancing?" He asked and I shrugged, wiping the bubbles from the glass.

"Um… basically as long as I can remember." I replied, drying the glass, and placing it in a stack on the counter. "my mom put me in classes when I was about five and then I just never stopped." I explained as I continued to dry. "Then I joined a musical theater group, started acting and singing and never looked back." I smiled. "I like dancing most though."

Nate smiled at me. “Well you’re good, from what I saw.”

“Thanks…” I replied.

“Really sexy.” He added and I felt myself blushing. I shook my head and avoided looking at him, but I could feel his gaze on me, like a thick air that wouldn’t leave.

“Okay, too far now.” I told him after a moment of silence. “I’m not some cheerleader that’s going to sit on your knee at lunch and giggle with my friends every time you call me cute.” I told him bluntly, and he held his wet hands up as a sign of surrender. The waitress grabbed the stack of glasses and returned them to the bar. As she left, she glanced at Nate and I and I smiled a little. “Or some waitress who’s clearly obsessed with you.” I mumbled and Nate scoffed, trying to suppress his laughter.

Nate looked over his shoulder and I followed suit, the head chef was giving us the evil eye and I put the cloth down on the counter.

“We’ve got about half an hour left so why don’t you go sit at the bar and chill out while I finish up,” he suggested. I nodded, leaving the kitchen, and heading to the bar. I looked out and noticed how busy it still looked, if possible, it looked busier than it was when I was attempting to work. I decided to just sit by Nate's car outside instead.

About forty minutes later, Nate made his way out of the restaurant which was still buzzing with customers and activity. It didn't close for another few hours, but another guy was coming to take over from Nate.

"Hey, sorry I'm late." He said, grabbing the bottom of his t-shirt and lifting it up, wiping the sweat from his forehead. I couldn't help but admire his torso for the brief moment he exposed it. I was only human, and he was very good-looking. I gulped awkwardly and felt a twang of guilt again. For some reason being around Nate made me have moments where I'd forget about Mason.

"Thought I'd find you at the bar…" He said, digging his car keys out of his pocket.

"You make me sound like a hooker." I joked and he laughed. I smiled at him.

"My boss wants to know if you want a permanent job…" He told me as he unlocked the car. We both climbed in.

“Hold on, what?” I asked, as he started to drive. “I was terrible.” I looked down to check my bag was still where I’d left it, which it was.

It was dark out now, but I preferred Fort Collins at night. Loads of the streets were lined with faint string lights throughout the year and they lit up every night without fail.

I stared out into the city as we drove, watching tired families heading back to their homes and couples walking past us on the sidewalks after their dates. It made me miss Mason — I’d barely talked to him all day. I wanted to hold his hand and have him hold me and take me on a real date. I wish I had my phone, so I could take a photo and send it to him, but he’d be asleep at this hour anyway so it wouldn’t matter.

“I’m not arguing with you there, you were not good.” Nate said and I lightly smacked him on the arm. For some reason I felt comfortable with him, comfortable enough to do that anyway. “Hey!” He exclaimed as he pulled out of the parking lot and started driving toward our street. “For someone who’s such a good dancer you have no coordination - how many drinks did you spill tonight?" He smirked.

"Excuse me, I balanced those trays perfectly!" I argued. "But there's not much I can do when a kid gets in my way." I told him, folding my arms across my chest, and laughing. I watched as Nate reached into his pocket and grabbed the photograph I saw earlier. He leaned across me, opening the glove compartment, and he shoved the photograph in and closed it.

"So, uh… Nate…" I started. "How come your family moved to my neighbourhood?" I saw his hands tense around the steering wheel, and I was sure I touched a nerve, but I didn't know why.

"Um…" He mumbled. Instantly the atmosphere in the car changed and I felt guilty for bringing the subject up. "It was just… a thing my parents decided would be good." He said, which didn't answer the question. He shifted in his seat and inhaled deeply and purposefully smiled at me, though it looked fake. "Because you know, moving to a new house and picking up your life for senior year while you're preparing to apply to college and get a football scholarship is definitely a good move." He said sarcastically.

"Ah… so you're going for scholarships?" I asked, trying to change the subject and ease the situation. He nodded and looked out at the road in front of us.

"Yeah, gotta pay somehow." He said and I saw him relax a little.

"Where are you applying?"

"Not sure yet… wherever will take me." He replied. I nodded and stared out the window. We sat in silence for the rest of the journey, he even turned the radio off so all I could hear were my thoughts. The intimidating feeling I felt when I first spoke to him was back and I felt out of place, like I'd crossed some sort of line by asking about his family. The journey across the city didn't take too long and when he pulled into his driveway we sat in the car in silence.

"Well… thanks." I told him. "For the ride home and for kidnapping me for the evening." I said, trying to joke and he smiled to himself. "I don't think I'm cut out to be a waitress though, so tell your manager thanks but I'm good."

Nate nodded and we both got out of the car. I looked at him as he locked up and started walking toward his front door. He turned back to look at me. "See you around. Maybe I'll come watch you dance again." He said, winking at me then walking into his home. I smiled and turned around, walking across the lawn before noticing I was still wearing his t-shirt.

What a weird night.

Chapter 6

RobinM110: *I miss you so much*

MPh2011: *Come to London!!*

RobinM110: *I'm working on it...*

I sat with Dad, tucked under a blanket as the credits rolled on the movie he'd chosen. I hadn't paid much attention; it was some action movie from the eighties which I'd probably watched before with him but didn't remember. We'd had a long talk about everything. He'd told me he and Mom had talked about the situation, and he was going to research musical theater majors himself to see whether or not it was worth spending four years on — which was more than I expected. He'd refused to let me move to London though or even look at colleges there, and that broke my heart, but I couldn't argue with him about it…

not again. I decided it was better to leave that topic alone for now.

"I know you love theater and dancing, but I want you to be okay when you leave." He'd said, pulling me into a hug as we sat on the sofa. "And it's so competitive, there's no way you can definitely get a job after graduating with a degree like that." I understood what he was saying, but I do wish he would just support it.

"I know." I told him, defeated. "But I love it," I paused. "You love your job, Dad. I don't want to be stuck doing something every single day that I don't like." I explained, yawning, and grabbing my dad's wrist, holding it in front of my face to check the time on his watch. When I saw it was 11pm I sat up slowly.

"I won't go to London," I started "but I'm not going to stop talking to Mason. I really like him, and I do want to see him one day."

"I understand." Dad said, rubbing my back supportively. "But you've never met him though, so of course I'm cautious." I nodded, and he leaned over and kissed the side of my head.

"I'm picking the movie next time." I added quickly and Dad smiled at me as I walked out.

After my shift at The Kingfisher a couple of days ago, I told Mom that I wouldn't go back. She didn't argue, but she also didn't stop looking for jobs for me… well, she'd stopped looking for waitressing jobs.

I hadn't spoken to Nate since then, but I'd seen him a couple of times outside the house or through my bedroom window. I sometimes spotted him looking at me through the window too, but I didn't mind too much. We smile at each other and carry on with whatever it is we're doing.

I opened my bedroom door and walked in. Changing into my pyjamas, I spied Nate's work t-shirt hanging on the back of my desk chair — Mom had washed it and told me to go next door to give it back but I kept forgetting… or at least that's what I kept telling myself. Something in me wanted to keep it, I wasn't sure why. After getting changed, I checked my phone to see a few messages from Florence.

TheGreatestFlo: *How's movie night going?*

TheGreatestFlo: *Convinced him to let you fly across the world to live with your boyfriend yet?*

I rolled my eyes at the messages but sat down on my bed and started replying,

RobinM110: *Not funny...*

She responded almost instantly.

TheGreatestFlo: *Sorry. Seriously though, how'd it go?*

RobinM110: *It was okay. Dad said he'd let me look at musical theater for college but is flat out refusing the whole London idea. I don't blame him, I guess it must be pretty weird from an outside perspective.*

TheGreatestFlo: *Dude, I'm an inside perspective and think he's right. Moving to London just for Mason is crazy and you know it.*

I sat and pondered her message for a couple of minutes. Was she right? Was the whole idea completely insane? It seemed like such a great plan when Mason had brought it up, but would it be a mistake? I guess they were right, I'd never actually met him and our entire relationship was set in cyberspace, but why did that make it any less real than if he were in New York or Nebraska or somewhere else in the US? I loved him, and shouldn't that be all that mattered?

RobinM110: *Maybe you're right... but I don't know how to tell Mason it's not happening.*

TheGreatestFlo: *Maybe you don't have to tell him it's not happening...*

RobinM110: *Come again?*

TheGreatestFlo: *I'm not saying move to London, but maybe you could go and visit him for a weekend? Go and meet him and see how it feels in person and if it's good then try and convince your Dad to think it through a bit more?*

RobinM110: *That's... not a bad idea*

TheGreatestFlo: *Oh, I know. I'm not just a pretty face baby.*

RobinM110: *Love you Boo*

I laughed to myself and put my phone beside my bed before standing up and walking over to the window. I pulled my curtain to the side and glanced over to Nate's bedroom and saw him sitting on the edge of his bed with his younger sister.

He had his arm around her shoulders, and she was crying. It was sad and I didn't know what happened, but it warmed my heart to see Nate comforting his sister. That was until I looked closer at Nate and saw him crying too. He wasn't sobbing like his sister, but I could see tears on his cheeks and instead of warming my heart, the sight broke it.

Nate reached up and wiped the tears from his face, looking down at his sister. He hugged her tightly and wiped her eyes then she stood up and left.

Suddenly, he looked directly at me. I didn't know what to do, we just stood there looking at each other and before I could think, he was walking over to his window. I expected him to close the curtains and shut me out for being nosey but instead he opened it wide. I opened up my curtains fully and slid my window up.

"Hi…" I said quietly. He gave me a weak smile and climbed onto his open window frame, ducking out and jumping the small gap between his window and my roof. I was taken aback but I didn't argue. "What… um…" I sighed, not knowing how to talk to him "Hi." I repeated.

"You said that already." Nate smiled a little, but I could see right through it. "So… this is what you see." He said, sitting down on the roof. We both just stared into his bedroom not saying anything, but this time it wasn't awkward or tense–it was sad, but it was comfortable.

I glanced at him then walked away. Grabbing his t-shirt from the back of my chair, I turned around to head onto the roof to give it to him, but he was standing behind me in my bedroom instead. He was looking around and suddenly I felt extremely exposed with him staring at the theater posters on my wall or the dance exam certificates Mom framed that I'd hung up. Playbills from musicals I'd seen were piled on my desk with my college brochures and clothes were scattered across the floor. Nate was getting a full glimpse into my life, and I wasn't sure how I felt about it.

"This is yours." I said, handing the t-shirt to him.

"Wait, did you wash this?" He asked with what sounded like a small but genuine laugh, running his thumb over the material, and sniffing it quickly as I smiled.

"My Mom did." I corrected and I sat down on the edge of my bed, patting the mattress beside me as an invite for him to join. "So... what happened?" I finally asked after an agonising pause. He sighed and looked down at the floor, not saying anything. The silence hung in the air and I bit my bottom lip awkwardly, not sure if I should prompt a response. It was late though, and I was tired and didn't want to annoy him.

"I'm sorry, I shouldn't have asked, I'm totally overstepping my boundaries." I retreated. I couldn't take my eyes off of him. His eyes were bloodshot and any ounce of confidence that he ever seemed to have was gone. He was just a boy who'd clearly been hurt by something or someone and that was all there was.

"No, no, it's okay." He said, wiping a fresh tear from his cheek. Whatever happened, it must have been bad for him to feel this way. I crossed my legs on the bed, turning to face him. "I- uh-" He started, sighing. "Jo sometimes has bad nights since it happened." He said and I made an educated guess that Jo was his sister. I listened intently and he looked up at me. I could see the sadness in his eyes, his beautiful dark green eyes. “The reason we moved here was because my mom needed a fresh start, but Dad didn’t want to take me out of school and move me somewhere new for senior year. My mom got super depressed and wouldn’t leave the house and barely got out of bed for weeks and when she did, she’d just torture herself.” He explained but I was none the wiser.

“What do you mean?” I asked curiously and quietly so neither of my parents heard us talking.

“Jo used to have a twin brother.” Nate said sadly, the tears welling up in his eyes. The breath caught in my throat and I felt sick with shock. “His name was Jeremy; he was the sweetest boy. He loved fire trucks.” He said, smiling at the last comment but letting a few tears fall. “He got sick and we had to use my very limited college fund to pay for the medical bills, but it didn’t help… nothing they did helped.” He said and I compulsively reached out and wiped the tears from his cheek. We both stared at each other intensely, and I was a little shocked at my own actions, but he let it happen. I could feel myself welling up listening to him, I can’t imagine how he must have felt.

“It was leukaemia.” He stated. I was lucky that none of my family had ever been seriously ill, so I didn’t really know much about this kind of thing, but hearing the quiver in his voice as he said it made my heart ache. “It happened really quickly. One day he was absolutely fine, playing with Jo in the garden and he fell off our tire swing and got really bruised. We didn’t think too much into it but then it just got worse which was weird because it was only a little fall. The next day, I was babysitting and he just didn’t want to get out of bed and I noticed he was really pale and the bruises were really bad so I called Mom and she told me to take him to the hospital, you know, just in case.” I didn’t take my eyes off Nate as he spoke.

“Then he kept getting these infections and one day in hospital he had a seizure and...” He stopped, clenching his fist and hesitantly I put my hand over his. “I miss him. He brightened up a room whenever he walked in and he was a pain in the ass, and he broke all my Lord of the Rings figurines when we were younger, but I loved him.” At this, he broke down and buried his face in his hands.

I sat and watched him, not knowing what to say or do. I wrapped my arms around him and held him there. It was strange, we weren't exactly friends and went days barely even acknowledging each other's presence, but now in this moment I'd never felt closer to someone. He was vulnerable and needed someone–he barely knew me but trusted me enough to confide in me. I wondered if he'd talked to all his friends like this but for some reason there seemed to be an intimacy to the situation that I couldn't imagine him sharing with someone else. Maybe a girlfriend, or a member of his own family, but another one of his jock friends? No way.

He wasn't obnoxious, stuck up, or a bully like I'd assumed. He was a guy who played football just like I was a girl who danced. He was a guy with a heart that had been broken worse than I could ever imagine.

"I'm so sorry, Nate." I told him as he leaned into my shoulder and I kept my arms wrapped around him. My cheek rested against the side of his head, and his hair was soft against my skin. A few minutes past and we stayed there silently. Eventually he sat up and looked at me, wiping his eyes and I stood up and grabbed a box of tissues I kept on my desk, handing him a few. I sat back down as he smiled weakly at me.

"My Mom wouldn't get out of bed, then when she did, she was just sitting in his empty room. Eventually my dad talked her into moving. When he told us, it felt like he was trying to just move on and pretend none of it ever happened and that Jeremy never existed, and I honestly was really angry." He continued to explain. I nodded along, showing him I was still listening. "But then I realised that Mom was practically broken, and I knew he was doing it for her. She just couldn't live in that house anymore," He paused, "so I sucked it up, buried the grief and helped my dad sort everything out for the new house. We still have all of Jeremy's things, but they're packed away in the basement. My dad and I couldn't throw out his stuff, but we're getting there. One day I think we'll donate them, but that's my parent's decision. And Jo's."

I couldn't imagine how hard it must have been for Nate to shut his grief away and move on the way he had. I was an only child, I'd never know what it was like to have a sibling and love someone in that way, and I couldn't begin to imagine how much hurt he must have been feeling these last few months.

"I haven't really talked about this before. Actually, I never talk to anyone like this," He admitted, and I stared at him intently. "You kind of… bring it out of me somehow." The way he looked at me made my insides stir, and I finally understood why so many girls seemed to fall at his feet. His effortlessly perfect brown hair; that stare that made me feel weak and the genuine sincerity he had whenever he spoke, even when he was joking. I felt angry at myself for judging him so quickly, as if being the quarterback immediately made him someone I'd hate, and I'd been shallow enough to believe it. "Sorry…" He said and I realised I'd just been staring at him.

"No, no, don't be!" I told him honestly. "I'm glad I could be here for you." I admitted, fiddling with my hair nervously in my hands. "I'm really sorry that happened to you and your family." I said, unsure of what to say.

"It was a few months ago now. But some nights are difficult for Jo and it kind of brings it all back. I think it was good for us to move here for my mom though, especially since your parents have been so nice, but even so, it doesn't get easier." He explained and I listened silently. "I've just had to be so strong for them, so I don't really get many moments of grief myself." He admitted and I felt for him. "I miss him a lot."

"I can imagine" I told him. "I mean, I can't imagine… but I'm here you know, whenever you want to talk... if you do."

We snapped out of the moment when Nate's phone started ringing in his pocket. He pulled it out and we both looked at it. "Who's calling you at this time?" I asked, curiously. Glancing at my alarm clock, I saw that it was nearly midnight.

"Um…" He said, reading the name that flashed on his screen, "Georgina" he told me before answering the call and standing up, heading over to the window and staring through it into his bedroom as he began speaking. His voice seemed so different to how it had been talking to me. He was chirpy and friendly and… fake.

Georgina was part of his clique at school. Her hair was always flawless, her makeup was pristine even after gym class (but I suppose that's what happened when you didn't participate, she always had some sort of excuse) and her friends always crowded around her like sheep, following her lead. I couldn't imagine being friends with her, it was all backstabbing and lies and drama, and yet they all dealt with it because that meant they were "popular".

She and Nate had the classic head cheerleader and quarterback relationship throughout junior year, but the latest gossip was that she'd cheated on him. I wasn't sure though, judging by the way he was speaking to her it didn't seem likely. "I can't, it's late, Georgie." He said. "Anyway, I'm busy." He added and he glanced over at me. I couldn't help but stare. His eyes were still red from crying. "No, I'm at a friend's house." I heard him say and that made me feel happy, hearing that he considered me a friend. Either that, or I was just an excuse to not see her. "I'll talk to you tomorrow." He said, then hung up.

"Sorry…" Nate said.

“That’s alright.” I told him. The spell was broken between us and I suddenly felt awkward in my own bedroom. I think he felt the same because as I looked at him, he just looked around the room and shuffled his feet. Though, I didn’t want to be rude and ask him to leave.

Nate slid his phone in his pocket and walked over to my desk, above which my dance certificates hung on the wall. “These are impressive.” He said, reading them all.

Beside them I’d tacked up photos of myself and my friends dancing or performing in shows. Every time I looked at them I remembered the fun I had working on shows and performances — how it felt being backstage and getting into my costumes, the rehearsals and the laughs and drama and inside jokes that came from them, and the stress of learning lines and songs with only a few days until the show. It was a thrill I loved more than anything and having the photos to look at everyday just encouraged me not to quit.

“You really love it, don’t you?”

I nodded, shyly. “More than anything.” I replied sincerely, walking over, and standing next to him to look at the wall too.

“I wish I was this passionate about something.” He told me and I noticed him glance at me. I blushed a little, hoping he wouldn’t notice.

“What about football?” I asked. He shrugged.

“I like it, and I’m going to try and get a scholarship and play at college, but I wouldn’t say I’m passionate about it.”

“I thought all high school jocks were passionate about football.” I joked, and he shot a genuine but weak smile at me.

His attention moved away from the wall, and he focussed on me. “Is that how you see me? As some high school jock?”

“Well… you are.” I told him with a small shrug, moving away from the desk and leaning back against the end of my bed. “I bet you guys see me as some nerdy theater kid.”

“I never really saw you as anything.” He said and I raised my eyebrow, putting my hand on my hip. “I mean…

I saw you… in the talent show with the glee club and stuff… but you never really made like a huge impact-" I stared at him accusingly. "Wait no, not an impact I mean, you weren't like-" I held my hand up and he stopped talking. I turned and walked away, leaning down and looking under my bed, pretending to be searching for something. "What are you looking for?" He asked.

"A shovel to dig yourself out of the hole you're in." I snickered, standing up straight again and he smiled at me.

"Sorry…" He laughed and I sat down on my bed again. He reached up and rubbed his bicep with his hand and I stared at him. "You know what I mean," he started, moving over and sitting beside me. "You're obviously super talented but you don't make a big deal out of yourself. You just do your thing and love it but you're more talented than any of the cheerleaders I know." He explained. "Georgie does some twirl in a routine and doesn't shut up about it for a week - you do shows and amazing dances and no one even knows."

"I don't do it for attention, I do it for me." I said, twiddling my thumbs as a small smile crept onto my lips.

"And that's why you're better than any of those girls." Nate told me and stared at me, looking me right in the eyes. His eyes were shining under the lamp light. I gulped nervously and my breath caught in my throat. "And um…" He added, shifting away from me and standing up. "On that note, I'm gonna go."

I watched Nate open the window and start to climb out onto the roof. "You can go out the front door, you know." I told him.

"You want me to wander through your house and have your parents see me walking out of your room at midnight?"

"Good point, window it is." I said. He began shuffling across the roof and I leaned out of my bedroom window.

Before he leaned over to his window to climb in, he turned back to me. "Are you busy tomorrow?" I shook my head at his question. "Okay well… I have a day off so if you're not busy and wanna hang out then just… throw something at my window." He smiled and then hopped over to his window, turned around and giving me a quick wink. I smiled to myself and closed my curtains, going to bed with butterflies in my stomach.

As I climbed into bed, Mason's name popped up on my phone screen with a message saying, 'Good Morning Beautiful'. He would have just woken up for work. I shut the phone off and ignored it. Instantly the butterflies were replaced with a pit of guilt.

Chapter 7

RobinM110: *Are you busy?*

MPh2011: *Just finished work, you okay?*

RobinM110: *Yeah, just wanted to chat.*

I'd spent the morning eating breakfast with my parents before Dad left for work. Mom told me she was going downtown to run some errands before heading to work, so I had the house to myself for the day.

Munchkin followed me up the stairs to the bathroom, brushing against my legs and meowing loudly. I grabbed my hairbrush off the shelf and fixed my hair into a tight bun before hopping into the shower. As I washed, I wondered whether I should take Nate up on his offer to spend the day with him. The idea made my stomach swirl and I couldn't tell if it was because I did want to or because even thinking about the possibility was making me feel incredibly guilty… but was I supposed to not have friends who were guys just because of Mason?

I held my breath and let the water pour over my face. Climbing out of the shower, I grabbed a towel and wrapped it around my body. I could hear scratching at the bathroom door and rolled my eyes.

"Munchkin stop!" I called but the scratching continued. I opened the door and he sat there guiltily, staring up at me with his big brown eyes and meowing. "You know you're not supposed to scratch the doors." I told him, looking down at the damage but it was impossible to tell what a new scratch was and what was old these days, there were too many claw marks to tell them apart.

He followed me back to my room and hopped onto my bed, curling up on a pillow and taking a nap. I gave him a quick scratch under his chin before my phone started ringing. I walked over to it and saw Mason's name.

"Hey!" I said enthusiastically as I answered. "What're you doing?" I asked, the smile present on my face. I pushed the speaker phone button and placed the phone down on my desk. Mason's voice now filled my bedroom.

“Not a lot.” He answered and the sound of his voice sent a shiver down my spine. His accent made me melt. “Just heading home from work, had to pop to town and do my food shopping.” He told me as I dried myself and picked an outfit for the day.

“You mean pick up your groceries…” I told him. One of my favorite things was correcting his British-isms.

“No, I mean do my food shop.” He argued and I heard him laugh into the phone. I wish I could have been with him right now, walking around the streets of London with his hand in mine. “Got any plans for the day?” He asked and I heard a loud siren in the background and the sound of traffic whizzing by him as he walked.

“Give me a sec…” I called from the other side of the room, pulling on my outfit for the day — a dark grey t-shirt with the words ‘I can’t, I have rehearsal’ on the front in big white letters and a pair of black shorts. I walked back to my desk to the phone and picked it up, pulling my hair out from the bun and glancing at myself in the mirror.“What did you say?” I asked.

"I asked if you have any plans-" He said, stopping mid-sentence. "Yeah, it's just down this road, then take a right at the crossing and you'll see a big white building, it's that." I raised my eyebrow, heading over to my window and opening the curtains. I couldn't help but glance into Nate's bedroom, but it was empty. I sat on my bed cross-legged and started petting Munchkin, putting the phone down beside me. "Sorry, someone needed directions." He said.

"I figured." I replied, listening to Munchkin purr against my hand. "Anyway, I asked if you have any plans for the day." He finally said. "What is it, 11am there?" He asked.

"No, it's 9." I corrected him. "But no," I started, looking over at Nate's bedroom. Suddenly, he was there now, and he wasn't alone. Georgina, the cheerleader who called him last night, was holding his hand and they were both sat next to each other on his bed. Suddenly, she grabbed his face and kissed him fiercely and my eyes widened.

Quickly, I ran over to my window and closed the curtains again. Getting up so fast startled Munchkin and he started meowing again.

"I uh-" I said, "I most definitely *do not* have any plans." I told him. There was no way I'd even think of spending the day with Nate now.

"Is that Munchkin in the background?" He asked, ignoring my answer. "Hello Munchkin." He said in a more high-pitched tone and Munchkin's ears pricked up. He meowed a couple of times. "Oh, I know, she needs to feed you doesn't she…" Mason said.

"Am I seriously sitting here while you have a conversation with my cat?" I asked, laughing a little and Munchkin meowed once more.

"Yes. Yes, you are." He replied and I could hear the sound of keys rattling. "Sorry, I'll just be a second." He replied and all I could hear was the sound of him fumbling around, doing who knows what. "So, how's everything with your Dad?" He asked finally.

"Okay I suppose," I told him as I laid back on my bed and Munchkin moved over to curl up on my stomach. "He really doesn't want me going to London… and honestly, he's not your biggest fan at the moment either." I admitted.

I heard Mason sigh on the other end of the phone. “He’s never been my biggest fan, babe.” He told me. “But that doesn’t matter. You should still look at schools here.”

“I am, but I want to take it one step at a time. I’ve still got the whole of senior year to sort this out.” I explained.

“No, you don’t. Applying internationally is a lot different to applying to schools in the US.” He told me.

“How do you know so much about this?” I asked him, curiously. I could hear what sounded like typing and I stroked Munchkin slowly, listening to him do whatever it was he was doing.

“Because-” He paused. “I’ve done my research. I want my girl here. I want to meet you.”

I sighed, sadly. “We’ll meet soon.”

Silence loomed between us and all I could hear was Munchkin snoring. “I’ve got to go babe.” He told me and I instantly felt sad. “But I’ll message you later.” He reassured me.

“Okay.”

“I love you.” He said.

“I love you too.” I replied and the line went dead.

I was abruptly woken up by the doorbell echoing through the house and I glanced at my phone, rubbing my eyes. It was 12pm, I must have fallen asleep cuddling Munchkin after my phone call with Mason. I sat up and noticed Munchkin was no longer in my room with me. Flattening my now scruffy hair, I walked downstairs to answer the door. I hadn't been expecting anyone, but for all I knew it was the mail man or a neighbour. I opened the door to see my friend Daniella from school standing there.

"Hi!" She greeted me with far too much enthusiasm for my liking, considering I'd only just woken up. "I haven't seen you in forever, how are you? Did I interrupt anything? You look tired, I didn't wake you, did I?" She said, firing the questions at me without taking a breath.

"Hi" I responded, a little less upbeat. "I'm good, no you didn't and yes, I was napping but that's fine." I laughed, watching her walk in the house as if it were her own.

Daniella was in the glee club and theater club with me but unlike me she only did them for fun — she wanted to be a doctor and I could understand why, she was one of the smartest people in the school. I stole a quick glance at her. Her frizzy black hair was tied up in a ponytail, and she wore a baggy sweater over a pair of shorts. She was very self-conscious, and never wore any shirts that hugged her figure, even though she had no need to feel that way. She was curvy, and she hated it, no matter how much I tried to convince her there was nothing wrong with that.

"I've been working so much on my internship," She started, and I walked her into the kitchen, grabbing two glasses and pouring us some water. "Seriously, this is my first day off all summer and we're already, like, nearly a month in, what's up with that?" Daniella was working with a group of high school students on a Medical Immersion Internship Scheme–something I didn't understand, no matter how much she tried to explain it to me. It was something about getting hands on experience in a bunch of different medical fields. All I knew was that it would boost her college applications to the top of any pile.

"Although, I can't really complain," She said as she grabbed the glass of water and took a sip. I'm pretty sure that's the first breath she'd taken between sentences since walking into the house. "I've been shadowing this pre-med student and seeing everything she gets to do, and it's been fascinating."

I led her up the stairs to my bedroom, listening to her talk non-stop about the different opportunities she'd been given, the pre-med student she was shadowing and how she thought she was really cute.

"Geez, why's it so dark in here?" She said, cutting off her rant as we walked into my bedroom.

"I was sleeping." I told her with a small laugh and watched as she walked over to the window and pulled the curtain open in one swift movement, revealing Munchkin perched on the window ledge giving himself a bath. The sunshine lit up the room and it took a second for my eyes to adjust.

Instinctively, I glanced over to Nate's bedroom, but his curtains were closed. Seeing this made a knot form in my stomach and I couldn't figure out why. Was it because I knew he'd had Georgina round and the last thing I'd seen was them sucking face so what more would have made him close the curtain? I shuddered at the thought, confused at why I cared so much.

“So come on,” Daniella said, sitting down on my desk chair and spinning it, so she could look in my direction. “What have you been doing the last few weeks?”

“Um…” I started, perching beside Munchkin on the window ledge and petting him. “Not a lot to be honest.” I admitted. “Lots of dance classes, been chilling talking to Mason a lot and researching colleges.” I listed.

I considered telling her about the shift at The Kingfisher, but thought better of it — that would just invite a lot of questions that would inevitably be about Nate and since I didn’t understand what was going on with him myself, trying to explain it to someone else would be nearly impossible.

Daniella clapped her hands together excitedly. “What colleges?” She asked. She was a great friend, but it felt like the only thing we talked about was school, so during the summer we only saw each other a couple of times because it always ended up that we didn’t have anything to talk about. I knew she’d be one of those high school friends that didn't stick around after graduation. She had ambition and drive, and that didn't involve staying friends with people from high school.

"theater ones mostly. AMDA, Julliard, places like that." I said. "There's one in London too which looks cool, but I doubt I'll go there." I admitted. "Just looked at it for fun."

"No harm in applying anyway." She said and I couldn't help but smile a little. She didn't overreact or tell me I was being stupid. She didn't even question why, she just supported the idea. That was nice to hear for a change.

Daniella stood up and walked over to me and Munchkin, kneeling down on the floor and petting the purring cat. I watched her and saw her eyes go wide.

"Uh- would you mind telling me why the reigning king and queen of high school are currently making out in the house next door?" and at this I shot my head round swiftly and we were now both staring at the couple.

Both of us kept our eyes locked on the two of them. "Oh right… Nate moved in a couple of weeks ago." I admitted. "...Did I forget to mention that?"

"Um yes!" Daniella said, slapping her palm to her forehead. "You didn't mention that or the fact that you're now calling Nathaniel Lewis 'Nate'? Since when do people call him that?" She asked and I simply shrugged, trying not to make this whole situation into a bigger deal.

"My Mom made me go and introduce myself to his family with her. They all call him Nate and he said I should too… so I am… mostly to be polite, you know?" I explained. Daniella had her eyebrow raised but still kept her eyes locked on the pair across the window. I felt intrusive just staring, but clearly Daniella didn't seem to think that.

"I did a trial shift at the restaurant he works at, so we chatted a little bit but that's about all." I said, avoiding telling her about last night when he'd been crying into my arms about his dead brother. Some things were too personal to share.

"Oh, *that's all?*" She said sarcastically as if I'd just told her something major. "When I ask what you've been up to that's the kind of thing you'd mention." She said, turning her attention to me for a brief second before looking out across the window. "God, are they ever going to come up for air?" She asked and I couldn't help but laugh a little, even if a small part of me felt sick at the thought of the two of them together. What was wrong with me? I had Mason, I was in love with him and happy and yet seeing Nate with a girl like Georgina made me want to compulsively throw a rock at the window and get them to cut it out.

"Uh oh…" Daniella said after a couple of seconds and I turned my attention to Nate and Georgina who were now looking directly at us. Georgina looked furious; Nate just smirked. I pulled my curtain closed quickly as if that would help in any way but heard Nate's window sliding open. Mine was also open.

"Take a picture nerds, it'll last longer!" I heard Georgina shout from across the way and Daniella snorted with laughter, she found it a lot funnier than I did. We both peeked out the window, easing the curtain to the side a little to stare at them. We could still hear them talking. "What the hell was that?" Georgina was asking Nate, gesturing over to my window furiously.

"What's the problem?" Nate asked and I could see the smirk still present on his lips. I couldn't help but stare at him. His smirk emphasised the small dimple in his cheek. He stared down at the petite cheerleader in front of him, running his hands down her waist. She pushed him away almost violently and he shook his head. "Dude chill, they didn't do anything."

"Don't call me dude!" She yelled and Daniella and I gave each other a passing glance. It looked like it was heating up over there quickly, and not in the way I'm sure it had earlier. "You always do this! You never take my side on anything!" We were keeping our eyes plastered on them, hanging on their every word.

"Your side of what? There literally aren't sides in this!" He said, exasperated. Munchkin started to shuffle and meowing loudly, stretching and easing his way out onto the rooftop out the crack in my window. His meows were almost as loud as Georgina.

"Yes, there are! There's my side, which is the right side, and the side of those pervert lesbians over there!" Hearing this, Daniella pushed the curtain to the side and opened the window wide. I could see the fury in her eyes and part of me knew I should stop her from doing whatever her instincts were about to make her do — but more of me wanted to see what happened. I let it play out.

"Yo, bitch!" She said and my eyes went wide with shock. Nate and Georgina both turned to us. "Trust me when I say that there's not a single part of you that this lesbian is attracted to, so why don't you get off your fucking pedestal, come back down to earth and realize the sun doesn't shine out of your ass."

I snorted and couldn't stop myself from bursting into hysterics. Daniella had never been ashamed of the person she was, what she wanted and to say what was on her mind, and this one took the cake. Georgina stood there speechless, and I could see Nate looking between the two girls.

After a moment of silence, he started clapping and I snickered. "Well said." He told Daniella, still applauding the show we'd just witnessed, and Georgina turned around and shoved past him.

"This is why I fucking cheated on you, I don't know why I bothered with you again." She said and I grimaced at the comment. A bit of a low blow. Nate simply shrugged and let her leave as she slammed his bedroom door behind her.

"That was incredible." I told Daniella, patting her on the back but I could tell she was shaking from the adrenaline of yelling at the head cheerleader. Not an opportunity that comes along very often. Nate leaned against his window frame, reaching his arm out and petting Munchkin who sat on the edge of my roof. "I second that."

"It *felt* incredible." Daniella said after a moment, laughing.

Chapter 8

MPh2011: *I really hope you can come to London*

MPh2011: *I could take you to dinner and we could see shows and go on real dates*

MPh2011: *You there?*

Placing my tray of food carefully onto the slightly sticky food court table, I took a seat across from Daniella. After her outburst to Georgina, which we were both still on a high from, we'd decided to come and get some food from the mall. The chair beside me squeaked across the floor as Nate pulled it out and placed his food beside me on the table.

Since Georgina had stormed out of his house, the three of us had chatted a little through our windows before Daniella had suggested that Nate join us for food. He'd been hesitant but decided to tag along. He'd sat in the back of Daniella's car on the way here, listening to us blast show tunes from the front seat. Daniella had been belting songs out as they came on, I decided to stay a little quieter — for some reason acting so carefree in a situation like that in front of Nate seemed impossible.

"So, I'm gonna mention the elephant in the food court," Daniella started, taking a sip of her diet cherry soda and picking around her fries. "The rumour around school was that she cheated on you but Timothy Dean told Jenny Fisher who told Phyllis Saxon who then told me that that wasn't true but obviously she said she did, so spill the beans, Jockstrap." She explained.

I listened intently, and followed her words easily, but when I turned to hear Nate's reaction, he just looked confused. I laughed and dipped one of my fries into the strawberry milkshake in front of me.

"What?" He simply responded and I took a quick bite of my food. I saw Daniella roll her eyes and I held my hand up as a signal to stop her from repeating herself.

"Let me translate." I said. "Basically, the gossip at school was that Georgina cheated on you," I started and saw Nate nod along, "but a bunch of people have also been saying that's not true. But then Georgina said she did cheat on you. So, Daniella's being nosey and just wants to know what happened."

"Oh... okay." Nate said. He watched me dip another one of my fries into my milkshake then reached over with one of his own and dipped it himself. Daniella raised her eyebrows at this, and I looked from her to the shake to Nate, who clearly hadn't noticed what an unexpected and unusual thing this was to do. He simply carried on speaking.

"I was going through some stuff with my family earlier this year," He started, and I felt the familiar knot form in my stomach. It had become a much more recurring feeling since Nate came into my life. "I was really focussed on that, fell behind in some classes and stuff and stopped paying so much attention to Georgie." He explained.

Daniella listened as if it was the most interesting thing, she'd heard all year. She was so smart and funny and such a proud person, but her kryptonite was drama and gossip. She loved knowing the goings-on of everyone around her

— even the popular crowd who barely even knew our names. Well, barely knew my name anyway. Everyone knew Daniella, she won all the academic awards under the sun, she was talented and into the arts but so smart it made even the nerdiest kids look like idiots.

"She decided she wanted to get my attention back and thought the best way to do that was to sleep with some hockey player from another school, I don't know the details." He said. "Anyway, it's for the best, we argue a lot and she's really not good for me."

"Okay then, forgive me if this is a stupid question but why was she practically eating your face earlier?" Daniella asked straight-forwardly and I stifled my laughter into my milkshake.

"I'm sorry?" He laughed.

"I think she means, why was she with you earlier?" I corrected Daniella and she looked eagerly to Nate.

Nate shrugged in response, grabbing his burger between his hands. "She puts out." He said simply, like it wasn't the most disgusting thing I'd ever heard a guy say.

I didn't like Georgina at the best of times, but that was a gross reason to stay with someone. Daniella threw one of her pickles, which she had discarded from her burger with disgust, at Nate, who swerved to the side. It flew past his head and landed in the frizzy hair of an older woman sitting with her family at the table behind us. None of them seemed to notice, and we all laughed hysterically.

This whole situation was so unusual. If someone had told me just a few weeks ago that I would be sitting with Nathaniel Lewis and Daniella eating lunch and having fun during the summer, I would have laughed at them and told them they'd gone crazy. This was so beyond the realms of normalcy that even sitting there now I had a hard time believing it was happening, and that I was having a good time.

"Okay, pig," Daniella joked, and Nate stared at her. She tilted her head to the side and eyed the boy up and down. I couldn't help but follow her lead and do the same, although I was far more subtle about it. It was only now that I realised just how close Nate was to me. If I nudged my leg just a little, our thighs could be touching, or I could gently brush my elbow against his bare, tanned arm.

"You're about the same build and size as my older brother. It's his birthday soon, he's gonna be like 25 or 26, I don't remember, so you're going to be my guinea pig for clothes shopping today, and you can't say no."

"Why can't I?" He asked, but he didn't seem particularly bothered by Daniella's demand. In fact, the small smile on his face seemed to welcome it.

Suddenly, the sound of a familiar voice broke our conversation, and we all turned to see Shaun Bennett, Nate's best friend and fellow football jock standing at our table, looming over us.

"Lewis?" He said, questioning the boy who sat with us. Nate looked from Shaun back at Daniella and I. "What're you doing here?" He asked.

Shaun stood there with another boy, slightly younger but not too much younger. The boy's hair was down to his shoulders and messy like it hadn't been brushed in weeks. He wore an army green beanie even though the weather definitely didn't require one, and he was wearing a slogan t-shirt with the words '*A Lannister Always Pays His Debts*' plastered on the front. If it wasn't for the striking resemblance of their facial features, you would guess they were strangers, but the pointedness of their jaws, their deep blue eyes and their identical noses were enough to show they were brothers.

Nate stood up and walked a few steps away from our table with Shaun, which in itself was enough to get mine and Daniella's full attention. We listened to their muffled voices, trying to figure out what they were saying.

"Why're you with those nerds?" Shaun snickered, judgmentally and I instantly felt sick. I saw his younger brother roll his eyes at the comment.

"Oh, uh…" We heard Nate stumble over his words and Daniella and I gave each other a curious look. "Just um… my mom, she signed me up for summer tutoring, you know, to get my grades up so I can stay on the team and get a scholarship." He lied. "Thought we'd get some food while we study." He added and Daniella and I both looked back at one another. She looked angry and ready to give another rant, but I grabbed her clenched fist and shook my head.

"Don't…" I told her, hushed and I couldn't fight the disappointment from my voice, although part of me definitely wanted to hear what she'd say. I felt like a fool — how could I have possibly thought that Nate would actually want to be my friend? He surrounded himself with the popular kids; kids I had known for years who had sure as hell made sure we all knew we were below them. He hung out with cheerleaders and football players — I was not one of them, and he knew it.

Letting go of Daniella's hand, I stood up, feeling embarrassed and hurt. Daniella followed my lead and without another word we left our food and walked away from the table, the food court, and from Nate.

He didn't even notice us leave.

Daniella had been ranting in my ear all the way from the food court to the parking lot about how stuck up the jocks in our school were. How they were so rude and conceited and how stupid it was that the idea of spending time with the two of us was too hard for their "tiny little minds to comprehend". I opened the car door and hopped into the passenger seat, still feeling hurt. It's not like Nate and I were actually friends. He'd spent one night revealing one of the worst parts of his life to me and suddenly that made us besties? No, of course not. The fact that I'd even had that thought in my head was idiotic. He needed someone to talk to last night, and I was there, that's it. He'd have chosen anyone else had they been around, I'm sure of it. At the end of the day, he was still Nathaniel Lewis and I was Robin Montgomery — two shooting stars that collided one day but are both still going in their opposite directions.

"You know, he actually seemed like a decent guy, that's the weird part! Normally I'm good at spotting the douchebags!" Daniella exclaimed as she started the car and began to drive in the direction of my house. "He should join the theater club. He's a good enough actor after all, had us both fooled." She mumbled and I could see her clutching the driving seat a little too hard. Daniella was an incredibly passionate person, but sometimes that passion burned a little too hard. "Oh well. He's just a fart in the wind as far as I'm concerned." She commented and I felt myself smile a little.

"What a lovely sentiment." I replied, turning on the stereo and hearing Daniella's musical theater mix begin to hum through the speakers. "Can I be honest with you?" I asked, twiddling my thumbs awkwardly.

"About?" She questioned.

"Nate." I said. "Last night I saw him crying with his little sister," I started. "He ended up coming over to my room and he cried to me about some stuff. We had like… a good talk. I won't go into what he said because it's not really my place, but I don't know… I guess I thought he was a nice guy. I thought he thought I was his friend…" I admitted, shrugging.

"Oh…" Daniella responded.

"Is that dumb?" I asked, knowing I'd get an honest answer.

"No." She replied, and I felt a little relieved. "If someone opens up like that of course you're going to feel that way. I guess this sucks much more for you then." She said. "But can I be honest with you now?" She asked and I nodded. "You knew who he was when he moved into that house, you knew what kind of guy he seemed to be… I'm not shocked about the way he acted today - to be honest, I didn't expect to talk to the guy after today. I don't think you should expect anything either. He only tagged along because I asked, and he was being polite." I paused for a second, looking out at the road.

"Yeah, you're right… like always." I said, giving her a smile to signal I was fine.

"Now, enough about that quarterback jerk." She said, reaching over and turning up the volume on her music. We sang along to show tunes on the ride home before Daniella dropped me off at my house.

As I walked up the lawn, I reached into my pocket and took a look at my phone for the first time since Daniella had come over. Over twenty notifications from Geeks Haven, including a string of messages from Mason.

MPh2011: *I've been searching scholarships and loans that you can get for London schools.*

MPh2011: *There're loads that will help pay for accommodation and all that kind of thing. I'll send you the links later when you finally come online.*

MPh2011: *Where are you anyway? It's not like you to not check your phone...*

MPh2011: *The only time you ever don't have your phone is at dance class and I know you don't have that today.*

MPh2011: *Well, wherever you are I hope you're having a good time, I guess.*

MPh2011: *Didn't mean to disturb you if I have.*

MPh2011: *Speak later*

I walked into my empty house and walked into the kitchen, grabbing myself a glass of orange juice as I typed out a response.

RobinM110: *Hey sorry, was ambushed by my friend and dragged to the mall, didn't have a chance to check my phone.*

RobinM110: *I really appreciate the thought, Mason, but money isn't the issue. My parents have been saving up a* *college fund for me basically since they found out my mom was pregnant so that's really no issue.*

RobinM110: *The problem is that it's on the other side of the world and my parents think the only reason I want to go there is because of you and to be honest they're not wrong. I love you and I want to be with you, but my parents don't see it as a practical choice, especially since there are so many amazing performing arts colleges here in the States.*

RobinM110: *You know I'd be with you in a heartbeat if I could, but let's face the fact that we've never met and no matter what I say to try to convince my parents, unless they know you're who you say you are then there's no way I'm going to be in London next year.*

RobinM110: *The only way they'd even think about it is if they could meet you. Make sure you're real, you know? Since I told my parents about you my mom has watched so many episodes of Catfish that her judgement is a little foggy.*

RobinM110: *I'll keep trying… but don't get your hopes up.*

I was sick of beating around the bush with Mason. Sick of getting his hopes up and knowing that inevitably they'd end up being crushed. I wish I could be with him; leave this city and this small little life I lead behind, but there's no way.

As I took a gulp of my orange juice, my phone started buzzing on the counter and I looked at the screen to see that Mason was calling me. I sighed, ready for the oncoming storm.

"I have an idea!" He exclaimed down the phone. "Why don't I fly out to see you? Your parents could meet me and the two of us could finally meet and then they could see that I'm… like… a real human being." He said, excitedly.

I pondered it for a moment. "That's… not an awful idea." I told him truthfully. Hearing his voice always made me feel better, that British accent was to die for. "But when? And how could you afford that? Plane tickets are crazy expensive, you know that."

"I've been saving up for a little while, I should have enough." He told me and I could feel the butterflies in my stomach. I hopped up onto the kitchen counter, staring out the window at Nate's house and swinging my legs a little. I felt giddy with excitement, knowing Mason could actually be coming to see me. I could hear him typing loudly on his laptop. "Okay, so, there's a flight out this weekend that goes to Denver… is that close to you?"

"Wait, wait, wait," I told him. "This weekend? Mason, you have to let me tell my parents first. Don't just get a ticket and fly over."

"I'm so sick of waiting around to see you though…" He said, and I blushed a little. It felt nice to be wanted by somebody. "I know… but… look, I'll talk to them tonight, okay?" I said.

"Fine. I wish you'd finished school already; you wouldn't have to ask your parents' permission on everything. If I wanted, I could hop on a plane and see you right now and no one could tell me not to."

"Must be nice…" I mumbled, mostly to myself. I longed to be out in the world, living my dream. Mason was only a year older than me, but it felt like he was so much further ahead in life than I was.

"I'm going to send you flight information in the morning, but I have to head to bed now. It's getting late here." He told me, and in all the excitement I'd forgotten about the time difference. Glancing at the clock on the wall I saw that it was just past four o'clock, which meant it was ten o'clock for him.

"Oh right. Good night." I told him, smiling to myself.

"Good night." He paused. "I love you."

"I love you too."

He hung up and I sat on the cold counter, staring out the window. I couldn't fight the huge smile on my face. Could it be possible that I was actually going to meet Mason after three long years? Could he finally hold me like he always says he wants to? Or kiss me like I've always wished he could? The pit of nerves was forming in my stomach, but I didn't care, it was a good nervous. The same kind of nervous I get when I'm about to go on stage. They were the nerves of anticipation.

Suddenly, I heard a knock at the front door and jumped off the counter. Munchkin brushed by my feet as I walked, and I remembered I needed to feed him. I tapped out a message to Florence on my phone.

RobinM110: *Mason might be coming to visit!!!!!!!!!!!*

With the smile still plastered on my face, I opened the front door wide only to be greeted by Nate, standing there with his hands in his pockets, looking directly at me. My smile dropped.

"Can I help you?" I said bluntly, sliding my phone into my pocket and leaning against the door frame. Nate slouched a little, but even so he seemed to tower above me. "Here for some tutoring?" I asked sarcastically. Nate looked me up and down and I immediately felt self-conscious. I wish he wouldn't do that. I stared at him and he just looked at me, standing there with his stupid perfect face and his stupid perfect smirk.

"Okay, so you did hear that…" He said, looking guilty. "But can I just explain?" He asked. I leaned out the front door and looked from one end of the cul-de-sac to the other.

"Are you sure you want to do that? Out here? Where *anyone* could walk past and see you?" I asked, adding a dramatic gasp to the end of my sentence.

"Come on, give me a break." Nate said with a sigh and I rolled my eyes, leaning against the door frame and crossing my arms in front of my chest. "Look, I'm sorry, okay?" He said but I just turned my back to him and closed the front door in his face, pushing it forcefully so the stiff hinges actually closed.

There was no way I was going to give him the opportunity to try and redeem himself. He'd been a jerk and there was no way he could talk his way out of this one. As I took a few steps toward the staircase I heard pounding on the door.

"Robin please!" He called but I didn't go back. "I know you're still there; I can see your ass." He said and I turned around swiftly to see his hand poking through the letterbox to prop it open. I leaned down and saw him staring through. "There's the little lady." He smirked as he caught my eye and I stormed over to the front door, slamming the letter box shut.

“Stop calling me that!” I yelled back, kicking the door lightly.

“Only if you let me in.”

“No!”

“What do you want me to say?” He pleaded through the closed door and I stood there, inches away from it with my hand on the doorknob. I wanted to turn it and let him in, but I stopped myself. “You want me to say I’m an idiot? That I was a jerk?” He said and I rolled my eyes. “I panicked okay? Shaun’s a dick and it would just cause more problems if I told him the truth about why I was there.”

“And what is the truth?” I asked, praying he’d say the right thing — mind you, I didn’t even know what I wanted him to say. That he did want to spend time with me? That Daniella and I weren’t nerds who didn’t deserve his attention? I don’t know. I sighed and opened the door. He was practically leaning against it with how close he was. Now I stood just a couple of steps away from him, staring up into his guilty face.

Nate looked directly at me. "The truth is… I think you're kind of cool… and I like being around you." He admitted. "It's just… my friends are… I don't know…" He mumbled, rubbing the back of his neck. It emphasised his bicep and I stared at him for a little too long before looking down at my feet.

"Great explanation." I said, sarcastically. "Look, I appreciate the apology and everything, but I don't think we can carry on being friends." I told him honestly, as much as it hurt me to say it. He looked disappointed. "If your first reaction when you see someone from school is to tell them I'm just tutoring you then what would happen when school started?" I asked. "You'd walk past me in the hall and look straight through me, just like you always have, and we both know it."

"Is that seriously what you think of me?" He asked and I shrugged a little.

"We can pretend all we want, but this-" I gestured between the two of us, "us… we don't work." I said. "And you proved that earlier with Shaun." Nate took a step toward me and as he did, I stepped back, I didn't want to close this gap between us anymore. “That’s okay though, I mean… we were friends for what? A week or so? No big deal, right?” Even as I said it, I felt myself hurt. It had felt like a big deal to me, no matter how much I pretended. Last night when he was in my room it felt like we were the only two people on the planet and to lose whatever that was did hurt me, but I couldn’t admit that.

“Right…” He said, backing away from me a little. “No big deal…” He repeated. The tension between us was clear now, and I wasn’t sure if we could go back to any kind of normal friendship — but that was fine. Even if we stayed friends it wouldn’t be for long, we’d be going to college in a year anyway, so what’s the point in making new friends now?

“Cool well… I’ll see you around.” I said.

“Yeah… see ya.” He said, turning away abruptly and sauntering over the lawn to his house.

A couple of hours after Nate left the house, my parents came stumbling in with bags of groceries. Dad carried so many he’d resorted to holding one under his chin. Hopping off a kitchen stool, I grabbed a few bags myself, walking them to the refrigerator and placing them down.

"Thanks sweetie." Mom said, placing the bags on the counter and fixing her appearance slightly. I started unpacking the groceries as I listened to Mom and Dad chat about some "moronic driver" who they passed on the way home.

I decided that now was as good of a time as any to tell them about the Mason situation. If he was going to come and visit this weekend, then I couldn't hide it from them for very long anyway. "Um, I had something I-"

"Sweetie, you're not wearing that tonight, are you?" Mom asked and I looked down at my outfit, completely oblivious to why she cared.

"...Why wouldn't I be?" I asked, curiously and cautiously.

"Honey, I told you, we're going to dinner with Caitlyn's family." She said and I stopped what I was doing, turning to her abruptly.

"We're *what*?" I asked. "Since when?"

"I told you last night." She said and I thought back to the evening. We had dinner together, I watched a movie with Dad, and I went to bed. I barely even saw my mother; she'd left me alone with Dad for the whole evening.

I shook my head. "I'm pretty sure I'd remember that." I told her. There was no way I was spending the whole evening sitting across the table from Nate acting like he hadn't been the biggest jerk to me.

Dad spoke up. "To be fair to Robin, you only told me after I came up to bed, I don't think you've actually seen her since then." He explained, taking a jar of spaghetti sauce out of one of the bags and placing it into a cupboard.

"Oh, well… I'm telling you now." Mom added and I rolled my eyes.

"I can't! I don't… have anything nice to wear." I lied.

"Don't be silly, you've still got all those dresses from that last concert show you were in… what was it again?"

"A Night at The Musical." I told her and she was right. The evening was a glamorous concert of theater songs and performances, some in costume but most not. I paused for a second, glancing out of the kitchen window toward Nate's house.

"Don't you think those dresses are a little flashy?" I commented, knowing that this wouldn't be a good enough reason not to go.

"Not all of them. What about that nice little red one?" She suggested and I watched her fill the freezer with a multitude of ice creams that were already starting to melt. "Look, just go and dig it out. It's a nice restaurant and it's Geoff's birthday so we're going to celebrate with them." She said.

"Do as your Mom says," Dad added. "That family have had a tough year, it'll be nice for them to have a distraction." I said and immediately felt nauseous. Did my parents know that I knew what had happened to Nate's brother? How could they?

"Be ready within the hour, please." Mom said. I walked out of the kitchen, leaving them to unpack the rest of the groceries and walked upstairs into my room.

Opening my closet door, I knelt down on the floor and heaved a large and heavy box out. It was labelled

'Costumes' and while they weren't all actually costumes, it was filled with clothes I wouldn't wear day to day.

I opened it up and started rummaging through, pushing various hats and shirts and a pair of neon green leg warmers to the side until I found the small pile of dresses at the bottom. I'm sure Mom wouldn't be happy if I didn't iron one for tonight, but I didn't care.

I picked out the red one she mentioned and unfolded it. Thankfully, it was a sort of stretchy material and hopefully when I put it on any creases wouldn't be noticeable. I quickly got changed and looked myself up and down in the mirror. The dress was a bold red and hugged my figure tightly. It stopped in the middle of my thighs and I grabbed the hem, pulling it down a little. I flattened the dress across my stomach and fiddled with it in various places as I stared at my reflection. I did like the way it looked on me, but I wasn't one for dressing up unless I was going to be on stage.

I brushed the tangles out of my hair and let it flow down to the middle of my back. It was wavy, and a little messy, but I didn't care enough to make more of an effort than I already had.

I looked over at my sneakers, resisting the urge to annoy Mom by wearing them then slipped on a pair of black pumps instead and grabbed my phone, putting it into a small black bag I only took out to special occasions. I still needed to tell my parents about Mason coming to visit, but I doubt tonight would invite a decent opportunity to bring up the subject.

I quickly touched up my make-up and went downstairs where Dad was sitting in the lounge watching a documentary about sea turtles. He was wearing one of his more uniquely patterned shirts. Since he wore plain suits to work every day, he liked the opportunity to show more personality through his variety of shirts and ties. Today he'd decided to sport a navy-blue plaid shirt with an orange and white striped tie. Staring at the ensemble for too long made me feel a little dizzy.

"Where's Mom?" I asked, clutching my bag tight as I felt my phone vibrate inside. I reached in and pulled it out, seeing a message from Florence that was simply a long line of question marks and exclamation points in response to my earlier message about Mason's visit.

"Upstairs, still getting ready." He replied. I took a seat beside him and stared at the TV. A turtle swam by the camera gracefully as the British voice-over started talking about how long they could hold their breath underwater. Hearing the voice reminded me of Mason.

"Dad…" I started. "If Mason came to visit, would you reconsider the London thing?" I asked. "Like, if you were there, and you could see he was real and a good guy?" At this, I heard Dad sigh a little and he didn't take his eyes off the TV.

"I don't know Robin…" He said. "Me or your mother would definitely have to meet this boy with you. You may be certain he is who he says, but there's always a chance." He explained and I nodded. "But…" He stopped and I could practically see the cogs turning in his head as he thought it all through. "I suppose he can come and visit."

"Holy shit, really?" I asked, excited.

“Swear jar!” He said, “and only if you get a job for the rest of the summer.” He said, looking at me now. His eyes were stern, and I could tell he was deadly serious.

“Fine! Yes! Deal!” I said, unable to contain my excitement as I fell forward into him on the couch and hugged him tight. “You won’t regret this, thank you, thank you!”

“I hope you’re right.” He said, patting my back before standing up and turning off the TV.

He walked into the hallway and I heard my mom’s footsteps coming down the stairs. I followed his lead, grabbing my bag and heading for the front door. Even dinner with Nate couldn’t ruin this evening now.

Chapter 9

RobinM110: *My Dad said you can visit... but only when I get a job.*

RobinM110: *So, don't come this weekend. I'll let you know more when I can.*

RobinM110: *I love you*

As I walked with my parents across the lawn to Nate's house, I stared down at my phone, eagerly searching the local job website for anything I could possibly do. If getting a job was what it took for my parents to let Mason visit, then that was exactly what I would do. There were tons of babysitting jobs, but after my experience at The Kingfisher with all the screaming children, I'm not sure that best suited my abilities. There were summer tutors but only for subjects in which I had passable grades and definitely wasn't smart enough to tutor someone else in, then there were the classic waitress or barista jobs. I thought about working in a clothing store that was a short walk from my house, but I didn't know anything about fashion, and the idea of trying to advise anyone on what they should wear didn't seem very suited to me.

Paying too much attention to my phone, I stumbled a little over a decorative rock that lined the pathway up to Nate's front door. I caught myself before falling over and Mom looked at me disapprovingly. "Give it here." She said, holding out her hand.

"What?" I asked.

"The phone. You're going to be polite tonight and actually enjoy this dinner. You can have it back at the end of the meal." She instructed and I rolled my eyes, shutting the phone off and reluctantly handing it over. She tucked it into her own bag, and I watched Dad knock on the door. I stood behind the two of them, attempting to hide myself from any attention or awkward formalities.

Geoff opened the door with a smile on his face. "Hey" he said, gesturing for us to head into the house. "Sorry, we just need to get Davey ready, he's refusing to wear shoes that match." He explained and I noticed Nate's younger brother fidgeting on the sofa as his mother attempted to put his shoes on. An old man sat beside them reading a book and I looked him over. Just like Geoff, he was almost the spitting image of Nate, other than the long grey hair, beard and wrinkles.

"Oh, we know the struggle." Dad said and Mom laughed, patting me on the shoulder. I caught a glimpse of Nate as he walked around in the kitchen but tore my gaze away, looking back at Caitlyn and Davey. "When Robin was younger, she refused to leave the house in anything but her Spider-Man sweater." Dad explained and I felt a little embarrassed, especially as Nate walked into the room at that precise moment.

"Spider-Man!" Davey shouted cheerfully from the sofa as his Mom still struggled with his shoes. He made little web-slinging gestures, jumping off the edge of the sofa, causing Caitlyn to sigh. Nate, without even acknowledging me or my parents, walked over to the two of them and held Davey still to help his Mom. I watched and couldn't help but notice how miserable Nate seemed to be — I was willing to bet I looked the same.

I watched as Caitlyn and Nate sat Davey still long enough to get a matching pair of shoes onto his feet before he jumped off and stumbled away. Caitlyn looked incredibly tired and definitely didn't seem in the right head space to be going out for a fancy dinner. Seeing her now, after what Nate had told me about their family, made me feel sad. She must have been so desperate to be happy again, but I doubt there was any way that could happen. I've always heard that losing a child is one of the most painful things a person can experience.

The old man stood up slowly from the chair, holding onto a walking stick that was leaning against the sofa beside him; he must have been in his 80s at least. He walked over to me and my parents as we stood by the front door. My parents were still chatting to Geoff, but I had completely zoned out. "Hello." He said, holding out his hand to me.

"Hi…" I said politely, shaking his hand. He turned to my parents and introduced himself to them too.

"I'm Albert." He said, "Geoff's father."

"It's a pleasure to meet you, Albert." Mom said, hugging him quickly before pulling away. I stared at him, seeing just how similar he looked to Geoff and Nate. It was almost like looking into the future, staring at this man who would without a doubt be exactly what the two of them would look like at that age.

"Dad lives at Shirleypoint, the old folks home on the other side of town." Geoff explained.

"Oh, how're you finding that?" Dad asked.

"Bunch of old biddies and codgers, the lot of them." He said with a snicker. "The nurses are lovely though. There's a strapping young lad who watches *Jeopardy!* with me every day. He's awful at the game but he's a good boy." As I continued to listen to him, I wondered what it must be like to reach an age where you can no longer do some of the fundamental things that people need to — like go to the bathroom, or climb into bed.

Albert seemed incredibly sprightly for a man of his age though and seemed to have some sort of sense of humour about the whole situation, but I wasn't sure if that was masking any real feelings he had. I wondered how it must have felt for him to lose Jeremy too, how it must be to have a grandchild lose his life before he did.

Caitlyn came fumbling over to us all, pulling her bag over her shoulder with one hand and gripping Davey's hand tight in the other. "Sorry I've taken so long, I really wanted to be ready before you guys arrived." She explained but Mom simply smiled.

"Don't worry about it, honestly." Mom reassured her.

"Nate!" Caitlyn called out through the house. "Grab your sister and let's go!"

I had barely noticed Nate leave the room whilst I'd been speaking to his grandfather, but I could hear footsteps from upstairs. They were clearly running around, and I could hear laughter from the two of them. Eventually, Nate came hurrying down the stairs with his little sister hoisted over his shoulder, struggling to get out of his grasp but laughing. I stared at him as he walked towards us all with her. He wore a navy-blue shirt with the sleeves rolled up to his elbows that clung tightly to his arms. His hair was swooped back effortlessly yet perfectly, and he wore a pair of old sneakers. I could tell they were old because the white that they were clearly supposed to be had turned a pale gray. I snapped away when he locked eyes with me and watched Geoff open up the door and lead everyone outside.

It was warm, too warm for a sweater but looking down at myself made me wish I'd worn something- no, anything else. I liked the dress Mom had chosen, but the way it clung to my body so tightly felt exposing, and I didn't like feeling exposed around Nate.

"Okay so, Geoff and I will take the kids and Albert in our car-" Caitlyn said, clicking the button on her car keys and unlocking it. "Nate, dear, you go in Kyle's car, there's no more room with us, but we'll see you there." She instructed and Nate and I both looked at each other with dread.

My parents and I began walking back over the lawn toward my house and headed up to the car. All I wanted to do was bolt back into the house and up the stairs, change into my pyjamas and get into bed. But no, I had to spend the whole evening enduring this torture. I could hear Nate mumbling to his Mom but couldn't figure out what he was saying. When we reached the car, I turned back to look at him and he jogged over to us to catch up.

"Sorry about that." He said to my parents, barely acknowledging me. We all climbed into the car, which was much newer and in a better condition than Nate's family car. All Dad ever wanted was a nice new car, and when he became a lawyer and started making money, this was one of the first things he bought. He got it washed once a week and never let anyone eat or drink inside it. Dad wasn't an uptight person with most things, but this car was like a second child to him — seriously, he named it Lucy.

Nate and I perched in the back seat and I kept myself almost glued to the door to keep as far away as possible. I stared out the window, refusing to even look at him. I was still annoyed about how he'd acted earlier that day, treating me like I was beneath him in some way, like he was embarrassed of me. Part of me hoped we'd bump into one of his friends just to see how he'd end up trying to play this one off.

"Your Mom told us you'd be able to give us directions to this place, Nate, we've never been." Mom said, reaching around her chair and tucking her bag down beside my feet on the floor.

"Oh, right, sure, it's just downtown." Nate said. I couldn't help but glance over at him when he spoke, explaining to Dad where to go while at the same time complimenting him on his choice of car, saying how much he'd wish he could drive something like this. We drove in the direction he instructed, and we both locked eyes again quickly. He looked like he was on edge, but also a little sad at the same time. I couldn't help but wonder if he was thinking about me.

The restaurant we ended up at was on the top floor of a hotel across the city called 'The New Waverley'. To get in, you had to walk through the huge, dimly-lit lobby to the elevators which were lit up with subtle blue lights. As we arrived at the top floor, we stepped out of the elevator to the restaurant. Directly across from the elevator doors was a fish tank which stretched the entire length of the wall. It was full of tons of fish, most of which I'd never seen before or had only seen in those British documentaries Dad watches. I spotted what looked like the entire cast of 'Finding Nemo' — is a fish tank complete without them?

Davey went running up to the glass and pressed his hands and face against it, staring at them. I followed him and bent down beside him with a small smile on my face.

"Look, it's Nemo." I said, pointing to the clown fish which swam in front of us. I could hear Dad talking to a maître d' as we watched the fish swim. I stayed with Davey as we looked at the fish and Jo walked beside me to look too. "Which is your favorite?" I asked.

She looked intensely at the creatures as they swam around gracefully. "That one." She said, pointing to a golden fish, larger than the rest, with fins so thin and long you could almost see through them.

"That's a good choice." I told her with a smile.

"Come on, guys." Geoff said and I stood up and turned around to join the group, with Jo and Davey following close behind. Nate was staring at me and his brother and sister with a small smile on his face. It made my heart melt a little, and this time I didn't feel guilty. I didn't care that Mason would probably be angry if he knew that I was having thoughts like this. Right now, I cared why Nate, even with a smile, looked so sincerely sad, regardless of whether I was mad at him.

The two kids ran into the restaurant to catch up with their parents who were being guided to a large table beside a huge window that looked out to the city.

"You look really good tonight." Nate finally said to me, and I looked up at him slightly. I didn't respond though; I didn't know how. "Are you going to ignore me all night?" He asked, putting his hands in his pockets and shrugging slightly.

"Maybe." I replied.

"I'm sorry, okay?" He said. "I was a jerk, I know."

"I know you know, and you've already apologised, so can we just drop it?" I said bluntly.

"Fine." He responded, frankly. "But just for the record, I don't think being friends with you was 'no big deal' as you put it earlier." He added as we reached our families and sat down on opposite sides of the table.

The restaurant was classy and had exposed dim light bulbs lining the ceiling. Everything looked too new and perfect. The waiters and waitresses were dressed in smart shirts and ties and the bar was rammed with people dressed up to the nines and having drinks. Some people looked like they were on dates, others in groups of serious-looking business people (the types that wouldn't be out of place at my dad's law firm) and others looked tired from long days of exploring the city as tourists.

The night dragged on, especially without my phone, but I ended up sitting with Albert and learnt a lot about his life. He's a talker and it was interesting to sit and chat with someone like him. He fought in the Vietnam War and fell in love with a girl who was killed after they'd left the country.

"You remind me of her." He'd told me. "She wanted to be a performer like you." He said, although I hadn't said a thing about myself to him, so I did wonder where he'd heard it. "She had the voice of an angel, but I only heard it once." He had explained as we ate our meals. "We only spent two nights together before I had to leave. A few weeks later, I was told that she'd died. I didn't think I'd ever love anyone the way I loved her, but then I met Nate's grandmother, and she brought that spark back to me."

"You're lucky to have found love twice." I told him as I played with the salad on my plate with my fork.

"Not really." Albert corrected me and I looked at him. "Falling in love more than once is easy, you just need to open your heart to the possibility and find someone who makes you ache in all the good and the bad ways." He said, and I looked over at my parents who were laughing with Geoff and Caitlyn about something I hadn't been listening to. I wondered if any of them had loved someone else before they loved each other. "Do you have anyone that makes your heart ache, dear?" He asked, picking up a chunk of salmon on his fork and eating it.

It was a big question. I thought of Mason, probably asleep right now in London, with his alarm set ready to go to work in the morning and the silence from me on the end of his phone. I thought about him buying a plane ticket to see me, flying all this way to meet me. It made me feel special, like someone chose me and wanted me in their life. But I didn't feel an ache.

"I wouldn't say he makes my heart ache, but I think he makes it flutter." I admitted, with a small smile. "With like… excitement." I added. "Like he makes me feel special." At this moment, I caught a glance of Nate, who was chatting with Jo and leaning over to cut Davey's chicken nuggets. I don't know why but looking at him made me ache. I didn't like the feeling of an ache.

"A flutter is good." Albert replied. "But my dear, a butterfly that flutters its wings must always land at some point."

I didn't know how to respond.

Chapter 10

MPh2011: *That's so great! Get a job ASAP so I can come! Or come to me and visit the school too!*

MPh2011: *I'll look up tickets to London and university tours if you want.*

MPh2011: *I really want you here.*

As fascinating as it was listening to Albert all night, I was thankful when I finally got home. Mom gave me my phone back almost as soon as we got through the door and told me that it didn't stop vibrating all night. With a sly smile, I took it from her and headed up to my bedroom to get changed.

I checked my messages from Mason and grinned down at my phone. I wondered if it would be better for me to go to London rather than him coming here. Maybe I could take my parents, and they could see that the school was good, and I wasn't just going there for Mason. Or at least, I didn't think I was.

I walked into my bedroom and saw Munchkin asleep on my desk, snoring almost as loud as he meows. He's such a noisy cat. Just as I was heading over to him, I spotted Nate standing at his bedroom window, staring right at me. He gestured for me to open the window. I froze for a second, not sure of what to do, but I rolled my eyes and complied.

"What?" I asked him, tired and fed up.

"Touchy, little lady." He said, leaning his arm against the window frame and I instinctively stared at his tensed muscles.

"If you're just gonna start being an obnoxious jerk again, I'm really not interested." I retorted.

"Okay, okay, I'm sorry." He said. I grabbed a dark red scrunchy from my desk, manoeuvring it from underneath Munchkin's paw and tied my hair up into a ponytail. I felt Nate's eyes on me the whole time.

"What do you want?" I asked again.

"I just… I wasn't kidding earlier… when I said you look good tonight." Nate said, once again eyeing me up and down. I'd had enough.

"Can you stop doing that?" I asked him, and I watched as he climbed out of his window and jumped across to the small rooftop outside mine. Just like he had the night before.

"Doing what?" He asked, climbing through my window and into my bedroom. He stood inches away from me and I could feel my whole body tense up. After a couple of seconds, I moved away and across the room.

"Staring at me all the time like that. Like you're trying to figure me out." I explained.

"And what if I am trying to figure you out?" He replied.

"Well, just… stop it. There's nothing to figure out." Nate sauntered over to my bed as I spoke and took a seat on the edge, making himself comfortable as if I'd invited him in.

"Look, I wanna get changed and go to bed so can you just... you know… leave?" I said exasperated, gesturing to the window.

“I just wanna clear some stuff up.” He said and he patted the bed beside him. I continued standing and he sighed. “Last night meant something to me okay? This whole weird-ass friendship or whatever it is meant something to me, even if it hasn’t been long.” He began. “I won’t lie, okay, I’m attracted to you. After seeing you dance and getting to know you a little, it makes me wonder why I didn’t notice you years ago.” He explained, standing up and walking toward me.

My breath caught in the back of my throat and I didn’t know what to say or what to do. I just stood there with him moving closer and closer to me.

“When you said that this was just no big deal, it did hurt a little, especially after last night.” He said, pausing. “I feel… comfortable with you.” The words seemed sincere, and what I’d felt earlier when I’d looked at him at dinner was back, but so much more intensely. I wondered if this was what Albert was talking about.

“I...” I started, but I couldn’t find the words. He stood so close to me now that I could feel the warmth radiating off of his body. I stared up at him in a daze.

"Honestly, since you came to work with me that day, I haven't been able to get you out of my head, and seeing you over here every day makes me-"

"Ache…" I said, breathlessly without thinking. We stared at each other, neither of us daring to look away or break whatever spell we were under right now. In this moment, it felt like we were the only two people on the planet, and honestly, I didn't want it to end.

Suddenly, my phone started to vibrate against the wood of my desk where I'd left it and it startled Munchkin, waking him up. He jumped off the desk and sprinted out of the room, and we both watched him go. I walked away to close the door then looked back to Nate. He was still wearing what he had worn to dinner, but his shirt was unbuttoned a little and I could see his collarbone from under the cotton. I admired the boy in front of me, knowing most girls in my school would love to be in this position. It's not every day that the quarterback tells you he can't stop thinking about you.

I walked over to the desk and grabbed my phone. It was a text from Mason. It must have been about 5am in

London at this time, so I instantly checked it out of fear that something had happened to him.

MPh2011: *So, I realised it's going to be almost impossible to get the time off work so here's a list of flights you could get to come and see me. Convince your parents please. I need to see you.*

I was taken aback by the message, not just because it was out of the blue for Mason but if it was true, I'd have to somehow convince my parents to not only pay money for me to go to London and meet him, but for them to come with me and find the time off work. It would be nearly impossible. As I stared down at my phone, I'd almost forgotten Nate was still there until I felt him walk up behind me. His hand touched my arm and stroked my skin and I tensed at his touch, turning around and staring up at him as I pulled my arm away.

"You need to go." I said with an awful pit of guilt in my stomach. "I can't do this." I admitted. He backed off slightly, looking hurt. "I'm sorry, but I love my boyfriend so much and I can't give up on him before I even get a chance to meet him, I can't. With that and what you did earlier, you made me feel like crap, like I was nothing, like I was someone to be ashamed of." I told him honestly.

"Wait rewind, what do you mean, *meet* him?" Nate repeated.

"Well, I mean… he lives in England." I told him. "I uh- met him a few years ago online."

"You mean you're blowing me off for a guy you don't even know?"

"Excuse me, I know him better than anyone else. I love him. He's my best friend and he understands me. He's not ashamed of me like *some people*." I gestured toward him wildly. "He would never brush me off or make me feel like I wasn't worth his time or like he's better than me." I argued. "You can't just come in here, tell me you like me but act like I barely exist when we're around other people, okay? Especially when you were making out with your cheating ex-girlfriend that same day! Life doesn't work like that. And you certainly can't come crashing into my life uninvited and start judging me for the people I choose to love." My voice was angry but hushed, I couldn't let my parents hear me yelling.

Nate stood there, speechless. After a moment, he made his way over to the window and climbed out. He turned back for a second and looked at me. “You don’t choose love.” He said simply and I watched him hop over to the window ledge and make his way back into his bedroom, closing the curtain and shutting me out.

What a mess.

Chapter 11

RobinM110: *I'll try to convince my parents to let me come to you, but I can't promise anything.*

MPh2011: *I need to see you. I need you in my life and I'm sick of waiting. Promise me you'll come.*

RobinM110: *Fine. I promise.*

It had been days since I'd spoken to Nate or even seen him. I'd barely left the house except for dance classes, and he never opened his curtains. Without simply going to his house, there was no way we were going to cross paths, and that thought hurt me. When he was with me all I ever felt was a longing that I'd been pushing away since day one. I couldn't deny it anymore, not after what he had said and what had happened. I could lie to myself all I wanted and try to pretend I didn't care, but after spending time with him and learning the real him, I couldn't seem to let go.

He wasn't just some stuck up quarterback jerk who thought the world revolved around him. I didn't even know where I got that idea from — it's not like he was ever an awful person in school. Sure, he was a little obnoxious, never cared about education and always wanted to be popular with his friends, but did that make him a bad person? Of course not. There was nothing I could do now though. The damage was done on both our sides and I doubted there was any way to come back from that.

My attention had to be focussed on dance classes, finding a job, getting ready for college, and somehow convincing my parents to let me fly to London… this was going to be a long summer. A small part of me no longer wanted to go to London, it was all Mason ever seemed to talk to me about now. We never talked about shows or how each other's days had gone — it was just him messaging me details about the college or about flights. It was almost desperate at this point.

I sat with my parents watching some sort of soap opera that Mom had switched on while Dad sat reading through a pile of paperwork. I was on my phone, looking at the job boards. One advertisement was called 'Youth Entertainment Assistant' and I clicked it to read the description.

'Youth Entertainment Assistant required on Tuesday and Thursday evenings from 5pm until 9pm to help run youth classes at Fort Collins Community Centre. Looking for an assistant to join the team in organising and running our children's tap class. Dance experience essential, tap experience preferred. Please call 555-0986 or message Tiffany Offpen on Facebook'

Immediately, I opened Facebook and searched her name. Eventually, I found her and sent her a message expressing my interest. If I had to get a summer job, you'd better believe I was going to try and find a job like this. She wasn't online, and it was getting kind of late, so I doubted I would get a response this evening. I continued searching.

"So, um… I've been thinking," I began.

"Yeah?" Mom replied, not taking her eyes off the TV. Dad didn't say anything, he just continued reading.

“Well, Mason isn’t going to be able to get time off work to visit so I thought it might be fun for us all to go to London and we could meet him and I could see the college and so could you and maybe it would make you feel better about the whole idea?” I explained, talking so fast I could barely keep up with myself. Dad stopped reading and looked at me with the same look I’d seen a million times.

“Robin…” He started.

“I know what you’re going to say, but before you reject the idea completely could you please just… think about it?” I pleaded. Mom looked at Dad and I could see him soften a little. I’m sure he was just as tired as I was when it came to talking about this.

“We’ll discuss it.” Mom said eventually and just like that, they went back to what they were doing.

My phone started ringing abruptly and I looked at the screen. Florence’s name lit it up. I hit the green button and stood up, walking out of the room.

“I have great news.” She said in her thick New York accent.

“Throw it at me.”

"I'm coming to Colorado!" She almost screamed down the phone and I stopped dead in my tracks.

"You're *what*?!" I asked, barely containing my excitement. "How?! When?!"

I could almost hear her smiling on the other end of the phone. "My dad's been organising an event in Denver for some company and he said I can go!" She said, with a squeal.

"Oh my God!!" I exclaimed. "That's amazing!"

"Oh, also, I have another surprise for you!" She said, but before she could continue, our doorbell rang.

"Give me a sec." I said, walking over to the front door and opening it.

Before me stood a tall girl with curly dark brown hair in a baggy sweatshirt and jeans. A girl I had seen in hundreds of photos for years and was standing before me in the flesh. I looked at her, eyes wide, and felt my jaw drop. Her phone was pressed to her ear and in shock, I dropped my own onto the floor.

"Hey Boo!" Florence said, instinctively grabbing me and pulling me into a tight embrace. "Surprise!" She laughed and I felt myself almost suffocating in my best friend's hair.

"Holy shit!" I said, way too loudly, causing Mom and Dad to walk out into the hallway to see the two of us. For the first time in weeks I felt undeniably happy. "Oh my God, oh my God, oh my God!" I squealed, feeling tears in my eyes.

She squeezed me tight then we both jumped up and down like a couple of children. "You're so tall!" I said and we both laughed as I wiped away the happy tears. I always imagined she was around my height, but she was at least four inches taller than me.

"Wait… is that?" I heard Mom say, and we pulled out of our hug, turning to my parents.

"Mom, Dad- oh my God," I said, smiling so wide. "This is Florence! You know! *Florence!*" I told them excitedly. Florence walked into the house as if she'd been here a thousand times and gave both Mom and Dad a hug each.

"It's so good to meet you." Florence said enthusiastically. I could still feel myself welling up from the excitement and wiped my eyes, taking a deep breath.

"Um… and you…" Dad said politely. I could tell by the look on his face that he was having a hard time placing her, but I appreciated the effort.

"Sorry to just drop by but I thought it would be fun to surprise Robin and I really wanted to see the look on her face and I know that you probably think I'm some crazy stalker but I swear I'm not, and I've been responsible, I haven't just turned up on my own, I promise. My dad's outside waiting in the car, I wanted to come up on my own but he wanted to make sure that Robin was who she says she is, just like I'm sure you're probably relieved to see that I'm who I've said I am but- I'm sorry I'm talking so much I'm just excited." She rambled and I laughed, looking out the front door to the car that was parked on the street.

The man inside, who I recognised from pictures as Florence's Dad was staring at us and he gave me a quick wave. Mom was beaming, grinning from ear to ear. I loved how pleased she always seemed when I was happy.

"Well, Florence, why don't you and your Dad stay for dinner? We haven't eaten yet and I'd love to find out more about you and why my daughter is always glued to her laptop." Mom laughed and Florence's face lit up.

"My dad's got a meeting this evening to discuss the event he's in town for, but I'd love to stay!" Florence smiled. I looked over at Dad and I saw him relax a little. I think he had finally realised that Florence wasn't a threat of any kind. I loved him so much, but I wish he wasn't so cautious about my internet friends.

"Great!" Mom replied. "I'll start cooking when my show is over. Why don't you girls hang out until then?" She suggested and I nodded.

"I just have to go tell Dad what's going on but that sounds great, thank you Mrs Montgomery." Florence said, bolting out the front door toward her dad's car.

My cheeks were starting to hurt from how much I was smiling but I couldn't seem to stop. I had been friends with Florence for so long and to see her here was like I was dreaming. Like she wasn't quite real and I was hallucinating.

"This is so exciting!" I exclaimed, quickly picking my phone up from the floor.

“Did you know she was coming?” Dad asked, peering out the front door toward the car.

“Not a clue!” I said, honestly. “I swear, I would have told you guys otherwise, you know that.”

“How does she have our address?” He asked.

I thought for a second before answering. “She’s sent me a few birthday and Christmas cards before, I must have given it to her a few years ago, but I have hers so it’s not that weird.”

Dad paused, and clearly wasn’t happy about this revelation but I stared at him pleadingly. “Since she’s actually who she said she is I won’t be mad, but no more giving our address out to strangers on the internet, deal?”

“Deal.” I said, the smile still plastered on my face and I gave the two of them a hug. Mom headed back into the lounge, followed closely by Dad and I waited by the front door for Florence to come back. I watched as her Dad pulled away in his car and left before she turned back and ran up to me giving me another hug.

"How long have you been planning this?" I asked, laughing in disbelief as I closed the door behind her and led her up the stairs to my bedroom.

I heard her chuckle a little. "A few weeks. Just before the summer, I think. It was so hard to keep it from you, honestly you have no idea how many times I typed out a message to tell you then deleted it. It was so worth it to see the look on your face though. It was like you saw a ghost or something!" She explained as we walked into my room and sat down on my bed. Munchkin laid on the pillow and Florence lit up. "Munchkin! Oh my God, he's so much fatter than he looks on video chat."

"Hey! Don't say that, you'll hurt his self-esteem!" I joked as she sat down next to him and picked him up, placing him in her lap. He didn't even flinch, he just accepted the attention, as always. I couldn't help myself and reached in, grabbing her for another hug. "I am so glad you're here; I don't think I've ever needed a hug from you more"

"Dude, you have no idea how long I was sat out there in the car trying to hype myself up." She said and I laughed.

"When you told me Mason was coming to visit I was so jealous because I was like 'dude no, I've been planning this for weeks, don't steal my thunder'" She joked and I smiled weakly, laughing a little.

"Well, he's not coming so you don't have to worry about that." I told her. She continued to stroke Munchkin but stared at me intensely.

"Okay, do I have to go to London and beat him up? What happened?"

"Oh no, he just… can't get the time off work." I told her. "But I'd rather see you right now anyway," I admitted.

"But I thought you looooooooved him? Why wouldn't you wanna see him?" She said sarcastically.

"Because boys suck and he's being really pushy lately about me moving to London for college and honestly he's getting on my nerves and on top of that I've got Nate next door who's also driving me insane and I don't know what to do about either of them and I just want all boys to go to hell." I rambled.

"Woah, Boo, slow down." Florence said, picking up Munchkin and putting him down on the floor. He sauntered out of the room casually and Florence held out her hand. “Give it here.”

“What?”

“Your phone.” She said and I raised an eyebrow.

“You sound like my mom.” I joked.

“I need to see these pushy messages and make a judgement call.” She told me bluntly.

“No no no no no-”

“Come on, you would have showed me them anyway and you know it.” She said. It was true, normally if someone was annoying me online or if Mason was pushing his luck, I’d show our messages to Florence to get her opinion. She did the same with me most of the time too. The only difference now though was that she had full access to type out what she was thinking and send it.

“I promise I won’t send any messages, I’ll just read.” She reassured me, as if she could read my mind — and honestly, after this long being best friends, it wouldn’t surprise me if she could.

I resigned to the fact that I wouldn’t win this battle and handed my phone over. She opened it up and checked my

Geeks Haven account. I watched over her shoulder, re-reading all the messages Mason had been sending me these last couple of days.

MPh2011: *You need to get a job already and save up some money to come visit.*

MPh2011: *You're old enough to make your own decisions, just tell your parents you're coming.*

MPh2011: *You promised me you'd visit, I'm not going to wait forever, Robin.*

MPh2011: *We've waited so long for this; how much longer can we do this?*

MPh2011: *I just want to see you and be with you and finally hold you and kiss you.*

At the last message, Florence made a little fake gagging noise and I snatched my phone back. "He's just… passionate." I told her.

"Passionate or crazy?" She replied. "Boo, I'm saying this for your own good. Don't move to London." At that, I let out a sigh.

"I want to study musical theater though, and I want to be with him." I said, although my heart was pounding now that someone had seen these messages. I couldn't quite figure out why the thought of going to London no longer filled me with excitement, but instead left me with a feeling of dread.

"You can study musical theater anywhere. It has nothing to do with the school and you know it." She said, leaning in and putting her arm around my shoulders. I leant against her shoulder and sighed.

"I want to see him though, I really do. I want to meet him and finally find out if what we have is… you know… real…" I mumbled, feeling uncertain about my own words.

If I was being honest, the thought of Nate standing in my room telling me how he felt was still whirling through my mind. Since he'd come into my life, Mason had taken a back seat, and if I was being totally truthful, I think that's why I was starting to feel so guilty and adamant about going to London.

"Anyway, I don't want to talk about this anymore right now. I have a lot on my mind, I just want to appreciate the fact that you're here and have some fun." I said, chirping up and Florence smiled.

I stared at the girl sat beside me. She had been my best friend for what felt like forever. I met her a couple of years before Mason was even in my life and she had been there for me through thick and thin. Meeting her felt like a dream, and I finally felt entirely comfortable around someone. Unfortunately, I knew she wouldn't be here for long, and once again our friendship would go back to cyberspace. But now that we were together it made me think that maybe meeting each other more often wouldn't be so difficult — especially if I were to study in New York. That was my original dream… before Mason.

We sat for a while chatting before eating dinner with my parents. They spent the entire meal asking Florence questions about how we met, who she is and what she does. She was extremely polite and funny; it was hard to dislike her and even Dad seemed to enjoy her company. He asked her questions about Geek's Haven and how we met and, of course, if she knew anything about Mason. She answered as best she could without disclosing too much about my online life. I didn't keep much private from my parents, but I didn't tell them every part of my relationship with Mason, unlike with Florence. I didn't tell them how much pressure he had started putting on me about coming to visit. I wish he'd stuck with his idea about visiting me instead — that was short-lived.

After the meal, Florence helped me wash the dishes while my parents left to watch TV. I couldn't help but stare out the window above the kitchen sink that looked out to Nate's house. I could see into their lounge and Caitlyn was sat with Davey reading. I couldn't help but smile a little to myself at the sight. She was so strong to be able to keep herself together for her children after what they'd been through. I felt guilty staring into their life, because I knew just how hard it must have been for the whole family — which made me feel more guilty because Nate is going through enough in his life without me piling more problems on him.

"So, what're we going to do for the evening?" Florence asked as she washed a plate. "I'm here for about 4 days so I want to squeeze in as much time with you as I can."

"What about your Dad?" I asked curiously as I placed the clean cutlery back in its drawer. I wished she was here for longer, but I would take whatever I could with her. This was the best surprise I could have asked for, and there was no way I was going to waste time moping around my house about Mason and Nate when Florence was here.

"Oh, he's going to be busy the whole time we're here. He's helped organise some conference thing and has a very specific schedule he needs to stick to. Whereas my schedule is literally just 'surprise Robin' which, obviously, has already been checked off." She explained.

I looked at her and I couldn't put my finger on how I was feeling. I was so excited to finally be meeting her but at the same time, it's like we had always been together, so the awkwardness of a first meeting was just, comfortable instead. "He's going to be working from about 7am until about 10pm every night so I wouldn't be worried about that. Though it does mean that you're essentially my babysitter for the next 4 days."

"You realize you're older than me, right?" I laughed.

"Well yeah, but only by like… a couple of months." She responded with a shrug, laughing as well.

“Okay, well, I do have dance class tomorrow, but that’s in the morning and then I can meet you at your hotel or somewhere if you’d like?” I suggested.

Florence’s eyes lit up and she turned to me, splashing some soapy dish water on my face. “Oh shit! I want to see you dance!” She said excitedly. “Can I come watch?” She asked and I couldn’t help but smile. Florence was always so unwavering with her support of what I do, and I honestly felt like there was no way I could have met someone better than her.

“Of course. It starts at 9, I normally get the bus, but I could ask my mom to take me and we could come get you on the way?” I said and she clapped her soapy gloved hands together enthusiastically.

“Amazing! However, young grasshopper, that doesn’t fix our empty agenda for this evening.” She told me, rinsing the last plate and handing it to me.

I wasn’t sure what to suggest. My plan for the evening was to look at college websites and do some research for my auditions and applications.

"To be honest, my only plan was to research for my college applications and then inevitably get distracted by talking to you and Mason." I admitted. When I said it aloud, it made me realize just how mundane my summer had been so far.

"Sounds riveting." She snickered and I rolled my eyes, watching her take off her rubber gloves and place them on the counter. "I joke of course, I'll happily sit with Munchkin in your room and help you do college prep." She said and I smiled. Only a best friend would agree to doing practically nothing for the evening. "As long as I'm with you, I don't really care what we do."

Chapter 12

RobinM110: *I'm not gonna be around for the next few days*

RobinM110: *Florence surprised me with a visit, gonna spend time with her. Will talk to you in a few days.*

MPh2011: *Wait so you're not gonna talk to me?*

MPh2011: *You can't just ignore me, Robin.*

I sat in the car with Mom, driving me to dance class with the biggest smile on my face. This was the happiest I had felt in a while, which was strange since everything with Nate was completely messed up; Mason was driving me insane with his constant clinginess; and I was still unemployed, but having Florence around made me feel like none of that mattered. It's funny how much you can rely on someone without even realising, and I didn't know how much I needed her in my life to make me feel happy. I guess that's what best friends were for.

We'd spent the evening talking about going to college, and she'd made me feel excited about wanting to go to a New York University, like Juilliard or AMDA, just like I'd always planned, but there was still a part of me that longed for London. After finally meeting Florence, I felt like I needed to meet Mason in person. I needed to see if we had the same connection that we always had online. I needed to see if he made my heart ache in all the good and the bad ways.

"Have you and Dad had a chance to talk about going to London?" I asked Mom, curiously as she drove toward Florence's hotel. I figured I'd better find out what their decision was before I started looking at flights.

"Actually, we did." She said and I couldn't help but perk up. She didn't seem distant or like she was going to beat around the bush — which is what Mom usually does when she has bad news. "I've been researching this college and it's a very difficult school to get into. There's auditions and things and they only take about 30 students a year for their acting course."

"Wow, you've really done your research." I said, impressed that she cared so much to look it up. "There's auditions for all the schools I want to go to and I know RADA is very competitive, but Mason said it's a great school and what's the point in setting my goals lower than the best? There's no harm in trying, right?" I said, practically pleading for her to understand.

"I know, I know. When I applied for college, I only applied for the best art schools I could find. The apple doesn't fall far from the tree and all that." She said, but I could tell she sounded a little exasperated. "But you've been talking about being on Broadway for years, wouldn't studying in New York like you planned be the best option for that?" She asked.

"Not necessarily." I replied with a small shrug, though I knew she was right. What better way to get your foot in the door on Broadway than to literally live and study on its doorstep? But I guess being on the West End would be just as good… if I even made it that far. "Anyway, we're getting way ahead of ourselves, I just wanted to know if there was a chance of us going to London. Let's forget about the school for now, you know how much I care about him, he's a huge part of my life and I want to meet him. Why can't we just go there for a few days, take in the sights and just take it one day at a time?" I asked.

"Well, your father won't be able to get time off work. His firm just got a huge murder case through and he's one of the leads so he's going to be at the office practically non-stop until it's done." She told me. I didn't like when Dad had to spend so much time at the office, the house was a little too big for just Mom, Munchkin and me. "But... I suppose, if it's just for a few days, we could make it a sort of mother and daughter bonding trip."

"Oh my God, seriously?" I exclaimed, unable to hold in my excitement. She laughed a little, pulling up outside Florence's hotel. "You're the best Mom ever."

"And don't you forget it." She said, "but you're doing all the organising. You find the flights, you find the hotel," She started, "at a reasonable price, and you make sure Mason is available. I'm there to take in the sights, drink tea, eat crumpets and make sure Mason is who he says he is." She said and I unbuckled my seatbelt and leaned over to give her a hug. "Now go get Florence, you're going to be late for class if we don't hurry."

Florence sat to the side of the dance studio watching myself and my class dance to that Spanish song *Despacito*. This was a group number that an agent would be watching us perform next week so it was important that we got it right. The agent was coming to watch Jason, who'd picked the song, so he was the lead in the dance which meant he also had a solo. This wasn't the first time he'd made us do this for various dance auditions, agencies and whatnot, but it was always fun — even if it was also intimidating knowing someone from the industry I wanted to be part of could also be watching me.

It was a much sexier dance than any of us were used to and a lot more advanced than the type of thing we usually do. I guess Miss Madison was pushing us for Jason's benefit. Why not show off what we can do, even if it's a lot harder?

As we danced, the music which was playing through the speakers from Miss Madison's phone cut off and was replaced by a ringtone. We all stopped, and she rushed over to her phone and shut it off. "Sorry guys." She said. "Take five, I should take this, it's Melissa." She told us.

Melissa was another girl in the class who was supposed to be doing part of the dance with Jason after his solo before we all joined the routine, but she hadn't turned up today. As Miss Madison walked out of the studio on the phone, I walked over to Florence who was sitting on the floor and I sat down beside her.

"You guys are so good." She said and I smiled. "Seriously, it's like watching a professional dance group, you all just move so well." I took a drink of my water and wiped the sweat from my forehead. "How long have you all been dancing together?" She asked.

"Well this group has been together for about 2 years now, with a few people coming and going here and there. Us as we are right now have been dancing together for about 3 months." I explained, taking another sip of water.

"Is this dance for anything in particular? A show? Or just funsies?" She asked.

"Okay, first off, don't say funsies ever again." I laughed, "and yeah, Jason's got some hotshot agent coming to watch him next week so we're all doing our bit to help him get representation." I told her.

"That's so cool!" She exclaimed. "Plus, he's ridiculously attractive." She whispered and I snorted. "What?" She laughed. I looked over at Jason who was sitting with Richard and Jeremiah, the other two boys in the group. I guess he was attractive, but I'd never taken the time to look — I didn't come to class to pine over the boys. "Like come on, that tank top is so tight I can literally see his eight pack trying to break out of it and I don't know about you but a sweaty boy like that just glistens under these studio lights."

"Stop!" I said, unable to contain my laughter, smacking her in the arm. Thankfully, before the conversation could take a more inappropriate turn, Miss Madison walked into the room.

"Okay guys, so bad news, Melissa has broken her foot so she's not going to be in class for the next few weeks." Immediately, Jason rushed over to Miss Madison and I could hear him asking what he was supposed to do now he didn't have a partner for part of the dance.

“Robin! Can you come here for a second?” She called and, confused, I stood up and headed over to the two of them.

“Everything okay?” I asked, even though I could see Jason was beyond worried at this point.

“Yeah, Jason’s a little concerned how he doesn’t have a partner but since you’re probably the closest in build and height to Melissa would you be okay being his partner?” Miss Madison asked. Jason looked at me pleadingly. I was flattered that she thought of me, if only because of my similarities to Melissa, but I couldn’t help but feel a sudden nervousness.

“Isn’t it a salsa though? I don’t really salsa…” I admitted.

“Well sort of, I like to call it a contemporary salsa, it’ll be fine. I’ll teach you the steps quickly and if you follow Jason’s lead, you’ll be fine.” She explained.

I thought about how I would feel if I were Jason. He must be terrified enough about this performance, especially now someone had let him down a week before it’s supposed to happen. I took a breath and smiled.

“Sure, yeah, I can do it.” I agreed. Miss Madison clapped her hands together triumphantly.

“Fantastic.” She smiled, patting me on the back then she walked into the centre of the studio. “Okay everyone, Robin is going to be taking Melissa’s place in the dance so I’m going to quickly teach her what she needs to know and we’ll have another run-through in 10 minutes so just practice on your own or in pairs for now and we’ll get this sorted.” She instructed and without hesitation everyone started working on the dance in their own parts of the studio and Miss Madison lead Jason and I to the centre of the studio where she began running us through the moves.

When the class ended, I felt a lot more confident about the dance, but I still had a way to go, so I promised Jason I’d work on it through the week for him.

“Okay Boo, what’re we doing for the day?” Florence asked as we left the studio. I quickly checked my phone and had a few messages from Mason asking how my day had been but I promised Florence I wouldn’t get distracted while she was here, so I popped my phone back into my bag and began walking toward the bus stop.

"I figured we could go to the mall, get some food and figure it out from there?" I said with a shrug, taking a seat on a bench. She sat next to me with her phone in her hand, typing furiously.

"Sounds good." She said, not looking up from her phone.

"Everything okay?" I asked, trying to peek a glance at the screen.

"Yeah, yeah, everything's good." She said, putting her phone in the pockets of her shorts and pulling out her purse. "How much is the bus?" She asked.

"Oh, don't worry, I've got it." I said and she put her arm around my shoulders and leaned into me.

"It's so nice to be here, it's cool not being in the city for a change." Florence sighed with a small smile on her face.

"Fort Collins is a city." I corrected as I saw the bus come round the corner and I held my hand out for it to stop.

"Fort Collins is basically a village compared to New York." She said, stepping onto the bus behind me.

“Touché.” I replied over my shoulder, smiling as I bought our bus tickets and took a seat.

She slumped down next to me and pulled out her phone and ear pods, handing me one. Tapping on her phone, she started playing some music that I didn’t recognise. She wasn’t much into the theater world like I was, no matter how much I tried to encourage her to listen to cast albums or live performances, but she also wasn’t into mainstream music. A guitar started to strum through my ear, and she stared out the window as we both listened. I glanced down at her phone to see the name of the song and saw a notification appear that read:

‘Geeks Haven: MPh2011 has sent you a message.’

“Why’s Mason messaging you?” I asked without thinking. Florence looked at me then down to her phone before flipping it over in her lap.

“Oh, it’s nothing.” She replied but it seemed she was avoiding looking at me and I could see that she was tense. I may not have been with her in person for very long, but I know when she’s hiding something from me — and this was no exception.

I crossed my arms and looked at her fiercely. “Spill.”

She let out a sigh of defeat and looked at me guiltily. “Okay, just please don’t hate me.” She started.

“What did you do?” I prompted. I knew that Florence had never understood my relationship with Mason. She was incredibly supportive of me, but she’d made it clear that being friends with people on the internet was a lot easier than having a relationship. She always said she didn’t know how I could be with someone when I wasn’t physically with them. I remember her telling me one night that relationships are more than just having a connection, like I always said Mason and I had, it was about the physical parts too. Remembering this just made me think about Nate.

“I just want to say, he messaged me first, okay? I didn’t do anything that wasn’t prompted.” She said, trying to defend herself even though I had no idea what she was even talking about.

“Florence…”

“He messaged me last night when we were hanging out asking if I could tell you to check your phone since you weren't replying to any of his messages," she started. "I told him that I'd surprised you and that you'd be busy with me for the next few days and he got all weird with me and said I needed to tell you to check your phone and that he doesn't like it when you don't message him back so I told him he was being selfish and that we've never met and we needed some time to ourselves." She explained. "I may have also told him he's being super clingy and needs to lay off." She admitted.

This wasn't the first time that Florence had got involved in mine and Mason's relationship. A few times over the years I've had messages from each of them telling me about their dislike for the other, and normally I'd be furious with Florence. Sometimes we'd go days without speaking because she'd crossed a line and upset Mason, but I always forgave her, because that's what friends do. This time though, I didn't mind. If anything, there was a part of me that was happy that she'd said the things she had. These last few weeks of Mason badgering on at me about London had been bothering me and I didn't have it in me to tell him that. No matter how much I wanted to finally meet him, she was right — he was being way too clingy.

I guessed Florence was bracing herself for some sort of onslaught of Mason defence from me. Her whole body seemed tense, she was barely looking at me, and she looked like she felt bad for what she'd said to him. So, when I laughed in response, she couldn't hide the look of confusion on her face.

"You're not wrong." I admitted with a shake of my head. "He's been… a lot to handle over the last couple of weeks."

"So, you're not mad?" Florence said after a brief pause. I wrapped my arm around her shoulders and pulled her into me.

"No, I'm not mad." I reassured her and she let out a deep breath. "I'm annoyed at him for messaging you. I'm annoyed at you for messaging him back, but I'm not mad." I admitted. I handed Florence her ear pod as the bus pulled to a stop outside the mall, and we climbed off with most of the other passengers.

We walked into the mall, and she said she was hungry for Chinese food, so we headed to Panda Express. "I do wish you hadn't hidden it from me though." I told her honestly.

"I know, but I didn't want to make you worry about it."

As we eyed up at the menu, I heard my phone ringing and pulled it out of my bag. I expected it to be Mason calling but it wasn't.

"Why haven't you responded yet?" The overly excited voice of Daniella said into my ear. I had no idea what she was talking about. Florence turned to me.

"Is that Mason?" She said but before I could answer she leaned toward the phone and said, "you're an asshole!" down the phone.

"Excuse me?" I heard Daniella say.

"I am so sorry!" I apologised. "It's my friend from school." I hissed at Florence and she instantly looked guilty. She mouthed the word sorry. "That was my friend just… making a joke, sorry. What were you saying?"

Daniella, seeming to barely give it a second thought, continued her questioning. “Like I said, you haven’t responded! Why?” She repeated.

“I’ll be honest, I have no idea what you mean. Responded to what?” I asked and I stepped forward behind Florence in the queue to order food.

“God, don’t you ever go on Facebook? I invited you like a week ago.” She said.

“Still not sure what you’re talking about Daniella.” I said and heard Florence laugh to herself in front of me. I watched as she ordered her food and browsed the menu board as I listened to Daniella sigh on the other end of the phone.

“The party at Rebecca Greene’s lake house tonight!” She said excitedly.

“...A party?” I repeated and Florence turned round with her eyes wide and huge smile plastered across her face. She looked almost like a super villain plotting their next evil scheme. “I don’t think I can make it. I have a friend visiting from New York and-”

"Bring her along!" Daniella said. "The more the merrier!" She encouraged and Florence pouted at me.

I noticed the server tapping her pen impatiently against the counter. I hadn't even realised it was my turn to order. "Oh um, the orange chicken please." I said politely.

"What?" Daniella replied.

"No, nothing, I'm at the mall." I explained. "Look, I appreciate the invite but-" I started before Florence leaned forward toward the phone again.

"We'll be there!" She said quickly and stole the phone from my hands. "Hi, Daniella is it?" She started and I just watched on unable to do anything. I loved them both, but they both drove me insane in their own ways — God only knows how I'd cope with the two of them together.

I watched as Florence got the information for the party from Daniella and shook my head. This was not how I'd planned to spend the day with her. As much as I was enjoying Florence being here, I didn't want my online life and my real life to collide. It would be too weird. How was I supposed to explain who she was? It's not like I can go up to my classmates and say she's a girl I met on the internet… could I?

After she hung up, Florence and I sat and ate our food. "Okay, so, this is exciting. We need a game plan." Florence started and I looked at her, confused.

"A… game plan?" I asked.

"Yes. We need to go shopping because I did not bring anything party appropriate with me on this trip and we can get you a cute outfit too." She said.

I looked down at the outfit I was currently wearing; some black leggings, my sneakers and a blue t-shirt that read '*Eat, Sleep, Dance, Repea*t'. To be fair, it was what I wore to dance class, but it wasn't far off what I would wear on a normal day.

"What's wrong with what I'm wearing now?" I asked as I looked over at Florence.

Her brown hair was perfectly curled in a sort of effortless way, and she wore a thin cropped hoodie and high-waisted shorts with sandals. Her look was casual, but a lot more stylish than anything I owned. She'd done her make-up too — a dark red lipstick and winged eyeliner so sharp it could cut someone. This, next to me, must have looked amazing since I still felt sweaty from class and had no make-up on at all.

“No offence, but your style is very… middle school boy.” She said, taking a bite of her chow mein. “Like… not in a bad way, it’s cute on you, but it’s not party material.” She added.

“I don’t know how to feel about that.” I admitted. “But fine, we can go shopping.”

“Yes! Follow my lead young padawan, I’ll make a jedi of you yet.” She snickered.

I shook my head and laughed. “What on earth are you talking about?” I replied.

“I have absolutely no idea.”

Chapter 13

RobinM110: *My Mom said we can come to London. Just need to know when you're free.*

MPh2011: *Amazing, I'll send you what you'll need to know*

MPh2011: *I love you. I can't wait to meet you.*

I stared at myself in the mirror and barely recognised the reflection. To say I was out of my comfort zone in this outfit was an understatement. After a lot of shopping and outfit rejections, Florence decided to pick an outfit for me without showing me. She said I needed to trust her, and I did… I wish I hadn't.

My hair was straighter than I've ever seen it, my make-up was done more than I normally would for a show, and that's a lot, and the outfit I was in just didn't feel comfortable at all. I wiped some of the dark red lipstick that Florence had forced on me off my teeth and pulled on the bottom of the crop top she'd picked out.

I was standing there in a dark red velvet crop top with a neckline that revealed slightly more than I was used to, and some black high-waisted jeans. Florence walked into my room after getting changed in the bathroom and stared at me.

"Fuck yes, girl!" She exclaimed.

"SWEAR JAR!" I heard Mom call up the stairs, and we both laughed.

"You look stunning." She said as I wrapped my arms around myself consciously. "Now you're supposed to say I look stunning too." She said, doing a twirl in her outfit.

Her hair was still curled but her makeup was darker with a full black lip and eyeshadow to match. She ended up buying herself a tight vest top which hugged her figure perfectly and some ripped jeans and ridiculously high heels.

"Well I thought that would go without saying." I replied with a smile, and she walked over to me confidently, pulling my arms down by my side and staring me in the face.

"You have an adorable body. Own it." She said forcefully and I nodded shyly. "Now come on, let's get going." She said, grabbing our bags and handing mine to me.

I looked down at my phone before I put it in my bag. No new messages from Mason, but we'd already said goodnight to each other, and he was in a better mood now that I'd told him I could come to London. I didn't mention I would be at a party tonight… I didn't want him to worry.

I quickly hugged Mom and explained that we wouldn't be back too late then we headed out the front door. I slammed it shut and walked, somewhat off balance, down the lawn.

"The bus goes from just down the street. It should take us just by the lake by Rebecca's house." I explained and Florence nodded.

As we turned to walk down the road, I noticed Nate's front door open and watched as he walked out. He stopped dead in his tracks when he spotted us. “Is that-” Florence started before I elbowed her in the ribs.

Nate stared at me intensely. This was the first time I’d spoken to him since a few nights ago when he admitted he was attracted to me. “Wow.” He said to himself, but Florence and I both heard him. He turned his attention to Florence, and I saw him look her up and down, like he always does with me and it made my face burn. I’m not sure if it was from anger or jealousy or what, but I didn’t like it. “Do I know you?” He asked.

“No, no, I’m not from here.” She said. “I’m Florence, Robin’s friend from New York.”

“How do you know someone from New York?” He asked, turning to me. I folded my arms across my chest and looked him in the eye.

“We met online… but you know… we both know I can’t possibly be close to someone I met online, right?” I argued without even thinking. It was an unnecessary dig, but it came out before I had a chance to stop it. Florence looked between the two of us and obviously sensed some tension.

"Anyway, we're going to some lake party, you wanna come?" Florence asked and once again I elbowed her in the ribs. "Can you stop?" She asked as she rubbed her side.

Nate laughed a little to himself. "I'm actually already going. Rebecca's, right?" He said and instantly I felt a sense of dread. Why hadn't it occurred to me that Nate would be going tonight? He was one of the most popular guys in school and if Facebook was to be believed, almost our entire junior class would be going tonight. I did not want to spend the whole night with Nate ignoring me because I wasn't good enough for him — I don't think my self-esteem could take it.

"You guys want a ride?" He asked and Florence said yes before I could even process what he'd asked. "Great." He said, staring at me intensely. I gulped and watched him head to his car.

We followed behind and I whispered to Florence, "the last time we talked we had a fight about Mason, and he told me he was attracted to me." I admitted.

"What?" Florence said, a little too loudly, causing him to glance over his shoulder at us briefly. "He likes you?"

"He doesn't like me. He just thinks I'm… I don't know. He's ashamed to be seen with me." I told her. I wasn't sure if I could properly forgive him for brushing me off with Shaun, but I also didn't want to be the type of person to hold grudges forever.

"He can't be that ashamed of you if he's going to be driving us to the party." Florence said. Maybe she had a point.

As we drove, I couldn't help but steal a glance or two at Nate. He'd clearly made an effort tonight with the way he looks. He wore a plain black tight t-shirt which emphasised the muscles in his arms, jean shorts and sneakers. It was a simple look, but his general demeanour and the clear effort he'd put into doing his hair gave him a very attractive vibe.

Staring out at the road, I tried to push the thoughts from my head. I wish I'd been able to sit behind Nate and next to Florence in the back seat, but Nate said his Mom didn't want his brother's car seat removed so there was one less spot. He had tried to clean the car since the last time I was in it though. There weren't any children's toys or crumbs in sight.

Nate took a turn toward town and I looked at him. "The lake is the other way." I said, but he didn't turn the car around.

"We just need to make a quick stop." He said and before I knew it, we were pulling into the parking lot of a convenience store. "Shaun asked me to bring some beers, so I won't be a second." He said, reaching to take off his seat belt.

"Wait, wait, I don't think that's a good idea." I said, instinctively reaching over and grabbing his arm to stop him from leaving the car. Florence leaned forward and let her hands rest on the seats.

"Me neither." She said and I felt a sense of relief before she added, "I'll go." and I shot my head round and glared at her.

"What? Why?" Nate asked and she snickered.

"Listen, pretty boy, people around this town clearly know who you are. Thanks to Robin telling me who you were, I stalked you on Facebook a few weeks ago and know you have connections in practically the whole of Fort Collins. People around here don't know me so it's much less likely I'll get caught, plus I've had a fake ID since I was about thirteen." Nate and I both listened to Florence and took a quick glance at each other, not knowing what to say.

"Um… well… be my guest." He said, admitting defeat. "I have a list of stuff Shaun wants." He said, reaching into his pocket and pulling out a neatly folded up piece of paper and handing it to her. Florence read it and rolled her eyes.

"Child's play. I'll be back in a few." She said, climbing out of the car and confidently walking into the convenience store like she'd done this a million times before.

"She's… certainly something." Nate said after what felt like an eternity of silence. I nodded.

"And that's why she's my best friend." I said, looking out the window toward the store to spot Florence inside and avoid any kind of eye contact with Nate. "You're not drinking tonight are you?" I asked, fiddling with my thumbs awkwardly.

Nate shrugged. "I might have a couple of beers, why?" He asked and I turned to him abruptly. I gestured to the steering wheel and the general interior of the car.

"Um, hello?" I said, as if it was obvious. "You're driving." I told him disapprovingly.

"A few beers won't hurt." He said and I hit him in the arm.

"Tell that to all the people who've died in drunk driving accidents, oh wait, you can't, they're dead." I said seriously. "If you're driving to this party and drinking then you better be staying the night or be having someone else drive you home."

"I'm not staying the night at Rebecca's house; I barely know her." He laughed, as if this was a joke.

"It's not funny. If you drive home and get caught you can kiss goodbye to any chance at a football scholarship." I explained. "You could hurt me or Florence if we end up coming back with you and worse off, you could, you know… fucking *die*." I ranted. As annoying as he was, there was no way I was letting him get behind the wheel if he was drunk. Someone had to take care of him.

"Okay, okay, relax." He said, placing his hand on my knee and the warmth of his skin against mine made me stop breathing for a second. "How about this: I have one beer then stick to soda for the evening? Deal?" He suggested. It took me a moment, but I took a breath.

"Fine, but if that one beer makes you at all at risk I'm not letting you drive home." I told him sternly.

"One beer isn't going to do anything, I promise." He said and now he was looking me in the eyes. I could get lost in his, the way they reflected the setting sun and seemed to stare so deeply into me. It felt like he could see every part of me when he looked at me like that. Suddenly, I heard the door to the car open, causing us to pull back from one another and Florence climbed in the back seat with three full bags of drinks.

She grinned, holding up the bags triumphantly, "who's ready to party?"

Chapter 14

RobinM110 *— No new messages.*

We arrived at the lake house and my body was numb. I felt like I couldn't move. There were loads of cars parked outside and there were so many people that I felt out of place, especially in what I was wearing. I just didn't feel like myself. Normally I found a reason to get out of these things, I'd tell Daniella I had rehearsal or a late dance class or a school project, then I'd sit at home and talk to Florence and Mason all night. Now, with Florence here, there was literally no escape.

"Let's go, fuckers!" Florence said, climbing out of the car and Nate raised his eyebrows at her, but I could see a small smile creeping onto his face. As strange as she was, it was hard not to like Florence. She handed the bags of drink over to Nate as I climbed out of the car and tried to find my balance on the uneven rocky driveway in my heels. I could see people all over the house. There were people on the porch hanging out and through the windows I could see so many of my classmates I couldn't keep count. The music was blasting so loud I dreaded going in the actual building and now that I thought about it, I barely knew anyone here. Sure, we were all classmates, but unless I was in some sort of group project, I just kept my distance. I doubted anyone knew who I was.

Florence grabbed two beers from one of the bags she'd handed Nate then passed one to me. "I don't know if this is a good idea." I told her, but she'd already opened hers and was taking a swig.

"Honey, Boo, love of my life," she started, putting her arm around me and leading me toward the party and away from Nate who had already started making his way in to find his friends, "this is what high school is about." She said. "When are you and I ever going to have the chance to come to a high school party together again?" She asked rhetorically before continuing. "This is where memories are made, so take a breath and let's smash this!"

I knew she was right. If I wanted to be on Broadway, I had to stop being afraid to put myself out there. I had to take chances and not shy away from experiences, and who better to spend my first party with?

I took a deep breath like she said, put a smile on my face and opened my beer. "Let's do this." I said and she squealed, jumping up and down then clinked our cans together. I took a big gulp, grimacing at the taste.

I spent the first part of the night saying hi to the few people I knew from school or spoke to at least. I knew practically everyone, just not enough to go up and say hi. I'd watched Florence play a few games of beer pong with a group of girls against Nate, Shaun and some more of their friends. Florence seemed to fit in with literally everyone she talked to; it was strange. I wished I could be like that. She had asked if I wanted to join in, but with stuff like that I'm much more of an observer.

As I stood and spectated the game, watching Nate with his friends without even realising I was staring, Daniella walked up next to me and pulled me into a hug.

"I'm so glad you finally came to one of these!" She said, taking a drink and I followed suit. I'd been drinking the same beer for about an hour now and the taste didn't seem to get any better. "Isn't it fun?" She asked, and I could tell she may be reaching her alcohol tolerance limit already. "Oh! I'm going to get us some shots!" She said and before I could stop her she walked away.

A few minutes later she came stumbling back to the beer pong table, where Florence had just finished a game, and put four shots down on the table. Florence snuck up behind me and poked me in the sides, shocking me and making herself laugh.

"Do I spy shots?" She grinned, grabbing one for herself and passing me one of the others. Victoria, a girl who had been playing with Florence, grabbed the fourth shot.

"Three, two, one, shot!" Daniella yelled and following the other's lead, I downed it in one, trying not to gag from the taste.

"What was that?" I asked, wincing from the sharp taste.

"Tequilaaaaaaaa" She sang happily, spinning around to the music and sauntering off without another word.

"She's fun." Florence laughed, picking up a plastic cup from the table that she'd topped up with something earlier in the evening.

"That's Daniella." I told her, taking the last gulp of my beer and looking around.

"Oh, from the photos of your shows! Yeah, I knew I recognised her." Florence said and I smiled. I loved how well she knew me and how much attention she paid to my life. It made me feel a little bad, because I doubt I would have been able to pick out any of her friends from a line up. Did that make me selfish? I don't know.

I walked to the kitchen and manoeuvred my way through a crowd of my peers and poured myself a new drink. I wasn't sure what it was, but I'd seen people drinking it all night so how bad could it be? I looked at my cup, full to the brim of a bright orange liquid and I took a sip and it definitely tasted nicer than the beer — sort of... well, like orange, almost like it wasn't alcohol at all. I realised how thirsty I was for a better drink and downed the rest of it before filling it up again and heading back to Florence.

"Let's go see the lake!" She said to me, grabbing me by the arm and pulling me through the crowd toward the back door and outside. There were speakers surrounding us and the music was blasting so loud you would probably be able to hear it across the lake. I stared out at the water and it was shimmering under the night sky. The great thing about being outside the city was that you could see the stars most nights.

"Woah, this is so cool." Florence said before taking a sip of her drink.

"Is it?" I asked, obliviously. It was just a lake, nothing particularly special about it to me. I took the last sip of my drink, not realising how quickly I'd been drinking it. I could feel my head getting fuzzy, but I didn't really care. I could feel my inhibitions leaving me and while I looked at everyone at the party, I realised that was the whole point. Practically everyone here was drunk at this point, screaming and dancing and having fun — why had I been so against coming to these parties? I felt… free.

"Robin, my sweet, my love, my con-fi-dant," Florence started, stumbling over her words and holding onto me tightly to keep her balance, but I could feel myself losing my own footing. “This right here,” she said, gesturing abruptly to the lake with her cup, spilling some beer onto the floor, “is *art*.” She finished, slightly yelling. I looked at her curiously.

“Art?” I asked before tipping my cup upside down and shaking it, seeing if there were any more drops of alcohol left. There weren’t. She took my cup from me and put it on her head like a hat and I laughed, almost uncontrollably, and she did too. I slumped down to the ground, sitting on the cold grass and Florence followed my lead, tossing the empty hat cup to the ground and resting her head against my shoulder.

“I don’t get to see this shit when I’m at home.” She explained. “You know what I see when I look out my window? Buildings. Buildings upon buildings upon buildings upon-”

“Buildings.” I finished and she nodded against my shoulder. “You can’t deny, New York is pretty beautiful in its own way though, right?” I asked.

I had dreamed of living in New York for as long as I could remember. I'd thought about having my own little apartment, rehearsing in a little studio for an off-Broadway show then making it big, dancing on the stage for some of the best musicals in the world with some of the best actors. Florence laughed at my question though, sitting up and reaching into her bag, pulling out her phone.

"It's beautiful for the first five minutes, if you have some sort of penthouse view and can see the whole city. You wanna see what I look at every morning out my window?" She asked, pulling up a photo on her phone. It was definitely New York, the view from her bedroom window. It just wasn't as picturesque as the arty photos I'd seen, or the movies made it out to be. It was gray, the sky, the buildings opposite, the smoke coming out of an air duct in the distance. Everything was dull.

"Oh…" I mumbled, not knowing what else to say.

"But this here," She said, gesturing once again to the lake. "It's nature, it's real. It's what the world was supposed to be, you know… drunk teenagers aside." She laughed. "It's fucking amazing, and you get to see it all the time. I mean, look at those mountains!" She pointed to the distant hills in the skyline. "This is art." She repeated. She was right, it was pretty spectacular when you looked at it like that.

Suddenly, she sat up and turned to me. "Enough of this deep shit, we're here to have fun!" She said, standing up carefully then pulling me up too. My balance was off in these heels and I knew I would regret them in the morning — my feet were already hurting. "Dance with me!" She said, pulling me over to where a group of people were dancing by the lake. I smiled widely and followed her, and we danced together.

We danced for a while, and as we did, I could feel myself losing more and more of myself to the music and the drinks.

A girl whose name I couldn't remember but definitely knew from school had brought Florence and I two more shots each as we were dancing. Florence happily took them, applauding the girl for her "sick beer pong skills". I guess they played together earlier in the evening. They started dancing together, jumping up and down and cheering to the music and I looked around at the crowd of people who surrounded me. I think something about the cold lake air and moving a lot to the music made the alcohol hit me hard and it was as if I'd suddenly had an extra six shots instead of two. All I knew was that my head would definitely hurt in the morning… and I was kind of okay with that.

I closed my eyes as I danced with myself, feeling the music and moving to the beat. I always lost myself when I danced, and this was beyond what I'd experienced before, and I loved it. I opened my eyes, looking through the crowd and I spotted Nate standing with a cup in his hand, laughing with Shaun. I stopped dancing and sauntered over to him confidently.

"What're you doing?" I asked accusingly, putting my hands on my hips.

"Um… enjoying the party?" He replied, clearly confused. I snatched the drink out of his hand and looked closely into the cup.

"Then what is this?" I questioned, taking a sniff of the cup and Nate just laughed, taking it out of my hand.

"Soda..." He laughed. "I told you, one beer then the rest is soda. I promised." He reassured me and I put my face in the palm of my hands and shook my head, embarrassed.

"I'm sorry, I should have trusted you." I said guilty, looking up at him with the best puppy dog look I could pull. He laughed again. "You make it hard to trust you. You're in my head all the time but I don't know if you're going to be like… Nate or Nathaniel, you know?" I explained, letting the words fall out of my mouth before I even had a chance to stop them and while I was well aware of what I was saying, I couldn't help it.

"I don't follow." He said, looking down at me, eyeing me up and down once again. His eyebrow was raised, and his hair was falling perfectly across his forehead. I felt a pit in my stomach open up again, but this time it wasn't guilt because of Mason, it was the ache I'd felt the other night.

"You-" I said, stopping myself, not knowing what I was going to say. "You do this *thing*."

"What thing?" He asked and I saw him look at the crowd and behind me, I turned around and saw Georgina standing there staring at us.

"That thing!" I told him, snapping his attention back to me. "Where you're either the really cute and likeable Nate who climbs in my bedroom and talks to me or you're the jerky Nathaniel who doesn't want to be seen in public talking to me." I said and he shook his head, snickering. "What's so funny?" I asked. He stared at me and I felt like he was looking into my soul.

"You." He replied with a small smile. All of a sudden, a familiar song began to play, and I heard my name being called across the crowd. Florence was staggering up behind me.

"This is the song you were dancing to earlier right?" She said enthusiastically. "Do it, do it, do it!" She cheered and I laughed and shook my head, embarrassed. She was right, this was the song. "Don't you want her to do her dance?" She said to Nate who I swore just winked at me.

"Yeah go on, show us what you've got, Montgomery." Nate prompted and I could feel the heat rush to my cheeks.

Before the rational voice in my head could stop me, I felt myself begin to move. Before I knew it, I was in the dance and people were moving aside to make room for me. I closed my eyes and ignored everyone, feeling the music in every move and blocking out the people attempting to sing along, and the chanting of my name that I heard from Florence then a few other people and as it went on more and more voices joined in. The dance wasn't the easiest to do in this outfit, it was much tighter than what I would normally wear to class, but I carried on, not being able to stop myself. My brain was telling me to run away because I was humiliating myself, but my body just wasn't listening, and I liked the way it felt.

As the song continued, I stopped and took a breath, it was a difficult dance, especially since I was a little drunk and could barely keep my balance when I was standing still. Suddenly, I heard cheering erupt from the crowd around me and I noticed just how many people were staring at me. I could feel my cheeks flush, but I couldn't help but smile. I looked over at Nate, who was staring at me like everyone else and I grinned widely, sauntering back over to him and I took his arm.

"Come dance!" I said and his face seemed to drop a little, and he looked around at his friends who were stood around us, but I didn't bother looking at them. All my attention was focussed on Nate.

"Uh, I don't think that's a good idea." He said but I dragged him closer to me and started dancing to the music. I held my arms around his neck and swayed my body against his, but I could feel that he was tense for a second before he relaxed into me. "You're… really something." He said quietly, laughing to himself. He started moving with me, but not as confidently.

"You're really hot." I replied, laughing. He snickered and rolled his eyes. I could hear my sober-self screaming at me in the back of my head. She was asking me what the hell I was doing and telling me I'd regret it in the morning. Nate looked down at me and held my waist as the crowd began to dance again and the attention stopped being on me. I felt slightly more comfortable, like it was only the two of us here. I stared up into his eyes and stopped dancing, losing my balance a little and holding onto his arm tight to keep myself standing.

"Yo, Lewis!" Someone called to Nate and I looked around to see some of the guys from the football team staring at us. "Beer pong table's free dude," they prompted and almost without a second thought, he let me go and walked away. Immediately, I felt sick, like I'd just humiliated myself in front of everyone and I could feel people's eyes on me again. I looked over at Florence, who was dancing with a guy from my English class and near them Georgina was staring daggers at me.

I was definitely going to regret this in the morning.

Chapter 15

MPh2011: *Saw the pictures, looks like you had a fun night last night.*

MPh2011: *Why didn't you tell me you were going to a party?*

MPh2011: *Why are you being so distant?*

I woke up at almost noon in my bed, being spooned by a snoring Florence. My head was throbbing, my feet were aching more than I'd felt for a long time and I felt like I was going to vomit. I don't remember how much I had to drink, but however much it was, was definitely too much. I could feel my stomach churning and all I wanted to do was go back to sleep.

I turned slowly to face Florence who had make-up from the night before smudged all over her face and I wondered if that's how I looked. I noticed she was wearing one of my t-shirts and pyjama pants and realised I was also wearing pyjamas. I do not remember getting changed last night… or getting home for that matter.

Gently, I moved Florence's arm from around me and climbed out of bed as quietly as possible. As soon as I stood up, the urge to vomit took over and I ran to the bathroom. I rushed past Munchkin who was scratching at the bottom of the door and I practically fell into the toilet, throwing up instantly. I held my hair back with one arm and rested the other on my leg as I bent over the toilet bowl. It was violent, so brightly orange that it hurt my eyes and the smell and feel of it made me feel light-headed but, once it was done, I did feel a little better. I could still feel my stomach churning though and knew this probably wasn't the only time I'd be vomiting today.

I took a few breaths and stood up, looking at myself in the mirror. Munchkin brushed against my ankles and let out a loud meow. I'd like to think he was doing it to comfort me, but I knew he only wanted food. My mascara and eyeliner from the night before had smudged over my face and my lipstick was faded, but not enough that it wasn't noticeable. I looked like every tragic woman in a rom-com that had ever done a walk of shame. I sighed, wiping the messed up parts of my make-up off my face with the back of my hand then grabbed my toothbrush and started brushing my teeth.

The taste of the mint toothpaste did not mix well with whatever taste was in my mouth right now. I wasn't sure what I could taste more — the alcohol, the sugary citrus of whatever I was drinking or vomit, but what was going on in my mouth was just making me want to hurl more. I quickly finished brushing my teeth and combed my hair through as best I could. It definitely didn't look as pristine as it had the night before.

I reached down and picked up Munchkin, who nuzzled into my neck and I stroked him under the chin. From downstairs, I could hear Mom talking to someone.

"You're a good boy." I heard her say as I yawned, still cuddling Munchkin as he purred against me. I felt someone walk up behind me and I saw Florence, yawning and rubbing her eyes. Without saying a word, she took Munchkin from me and started cuddling him, which he didn't seem to mind. He was a very loving boy.

"What a night," Florence said through another yawn. I shushed her and continued to listen to Mom.

"Let me make you some lunch, just to say thanks." Mom said to the mysterious good boy. Florence looked at me puzzled as she mouthed the words 'who is it?' to me. I simply shrugged and began making my way downstairs.

I regretted that choice instantly as I saw who stood in the doorway. Nate, with his perfect hair and perfect body and perfect face. God, what was wrong with me?

"There's the little lady…" He said with a smirk plastered across his lips. Florence followed behind me and Munchkin climbed out of her arms and wobbled his fat little body down the stairs, not unlike Florence and I as we dragged our hungover bodies down too.

"Please don't call me that." I mumbled, rubbing my head as I yawned again.

"He can call you whatever he wants after what you pulled." Mom said and I looked at her, lost. "Oh, please tell me you remember?" She asked and she let out a small but clearly disapproving laugh. She sighed, walking over to me and putting her hand on my shoulder.

“My baby’s first hangover, I’m so proud.” She said sarcastically. Nate laughed from behind her and I looked over to him again, annoyed.

“Don’t look at him like that,” Mom began, and I looked back at her as she pushed my hair behind my ear. “You’re lucky he drove you home last night otherwise God knows what would have happened to the two of you.” She explained, looking at Florence who stood beside me. “Now come on, let’s get some water and food in your systems, and Nate, you can join us too, I won’t take no for an answer.” She instructed as she turned to walk into the kitchen and reluctantly, he walked in and tried to close the front door behind him.

I saw him struggle to close it and walked over, slamming the door shut hard. “It just needs a bit of force.” I said then turned away from him and followed Mom and Florence into the kitchen.

“I can fix that, you know.” Nate said to Mom.

“Fix what?” She asked, pouring glasses of water for the four of us.

"The door, if you want." He said and my mom's eyes lit up.

"Oh, that would be amazing! Do you need anything, tools?" She asked, clearly as clueless as I was. Now I understood why it had been broken this whole time.

"That's fine, I've got everything back at my house, I won't be a minute." He told her. I watched him walk out of the house. I could see him through the window walking across the lawn and I couldn't help but stare at him. I vaguely remembered talking to him at the party, but I definitely didn't remember him driving Florence and I home.

"Um, you've got a little bit of drool…" Florence laughed, rolling her eyes at me.

"What?" I said, wiping my mouth quickly. Mom handed me a glass of water and I took a sip.

"Could you want him more?" Florence asked and I glared at her, hitting her in the arm.

Mom looked at the two of us disapprovingly. "Robin, sweetie, is that true?" She asked. I bit my lip awkwardly, looking down at my glass of water and avoiding eye contact with either of them. "Robin…" She prompted.

I hesitated. "Well… no, it's not." I said. "I mean, he's… nice… and like, yeah…" I mumbled, mentally slapping myself. "But it's fine, I'm with Mason." I said seriously.

Florence looked at me sincerely. "Yeah but, you're not. Mason's across the world, you've never even met him, and he's been terrible to you these last few weeks."

"He's been terrible?" Mom repeated. I could almost hear her blood boiling. "What did he do? What's he said?"

"Nothing!" I reassured her quickly. "Nothing, he's done nothing. He's just been a bit pushy is all. He really wants me to visit and I've barely given him the time of day recently because I've been busy with dance and Florence and stuff. He's fine, I just think we're a bit strained right now, but that'll be fine when we go and see him." I explained. I saw Florence rolled her eyes.

"Okay fine, I'll take your word for it," Florence said, looking out the kitchen window then pointing over to Nate who was walking back toward the house, "but I saw you guys last night. You're cute." She said and I felt butterflies in my stomach. Well, either butterflies or the sudden urge to vomit again… or both.

"Whatever, can we just stop talking about it?" I pleaded as I heard the front door open again as Nate walked back into the house. Mom was making sandwiches for us all as we talked and she invited Nate back into the kitchen.

"Have lunch and then you can do what you need to do to the door." Mom said with a smile, slicing the sandwiches in half and piling them onto a plate. She also placed some brownies on a plate, and I looked over at the food. As hungry as I felt, the thought of eating any food made me feel like I was going to vomit again.

Mom walked up behind me and wrapped her arms around my shoulders. "No laptop for a week by the way." She said and I turned around to her abruptly. As I was about to argue, I felt my stomach turn and I shot out of the kitchen and ran upstairs to the bathroom again, throwing up into the toilet bowl. I could hear Mom laughing at me from downstairs.

"ISN'T THIS PUNISHMENT ENOUGH?" I yelled from the bathroom and heard the three of them laugh at me from the kitchen. I sighed, wiping my mouth and standing up. I wish Nate wasn't seeing me like this. I walked into my bedroom to grab my phone and decided to call Mason. He shouldn't have been at work at this time. As it rang, I picked up my laptop from my desk to give it to Mom. I didn't have the energy to argue with her. Suddenly I heard Mason's voice on the other end of the phone.

"Finally talking to me then?" He said and I immediately felt guilty.

I paced around my room. "Don't be like that." I said.

"How am I supposed to be?" He asked. I did feel a bit guilty; I probably should have talked to him a little more lately. "You've been basically blanking me."

"That's not true." I argued. "Florence has been here, and we've never met before and I was just excited and wanted to spend some time with her." I explained. "Surely you can understand that?"

"I get it, but what I don't get is all the photos of you at some party all over Facebook." He said and I was instantly filled with dread. I sat down on my bed and opened up my laptop. There I was, tagged in photos from the night before. They seemed fine, someone had taken a really nice photo of Florence and I sat together looking out at the lake, but then as I scrolled through, they seemed to get worse and worse. One photo was of a group of us doing shots, then a photo of me dancing, and another, and another, and photos of me with… Nate?

"I am so sorry. It was Florence's idea; I didn't even want to go." I told him desperately. "I promise, the next time I go to one of those things, I'll tell you."

There was a long silence at the end of the phone. "I'd really feel more comfortable if you didn't go to any more parties." He said and I didn't know how to respond. "Then, when you come to university here, we can go to these things together and I can keep an eye on you." I guess it wasn't unreasonable for him to want that, right? I did lie, and the photos don't exactly show me in the best light, so I understand where he's coming from but it felt less like a request and more like a demand, and that made me uncomfortable.

After a second, I sighed. "Okay, no more parties." I said, defeated.

His whole tone of voice shifted in that instant, and he sounded upbeat as he said, "So any news on coming to visit?" I smiled weakly.

"Yeah actually, Mom said I could book some flights and we'll come for a couple of days." The more we talked about this visit, the less I wanted to do it. I guess it was the guilt from everything with Nate, but I knew if I just pushed that away for now it would be fine. I'd finally see Mason, and everything would go back to normal.

"Amazing!" He said enthusiastically. "I'll let you know when I'm free and then just book the tickets and tell me the details!" He said.

"Okay." I replied. "Well, my mom's calling me so I've gotta go," I lied, "but I'll let you know when I've booked tickets."

"Alright, I love you." He said. I hesitated before replying.

"I love you too."

Sitting with Florence in the kitchen, I looked up flights to England on my phone. Mason had almost immediately sent me the details of his work schedule, so I decided to just get to it. Florence stared over my shoulder at the flight times, giving me advice on the best airlines and deals. She'd travelled quite a lot with her Dad.

Since she was an only child and her mother wasn't in the picture anymore, she said her Dad took her all over the world while she grew up because he didn't want to be travelling for weeks without her. She'd been to England, Japan, Australia and everywhere in between and sent me postcards when we'd become friends. They're all stuck on my wall with my show photographs.

As we searched, my phone began to ring with an unfamiliar number flashing across the screen. I hesitated before picking up. "This is Robin," I stated, waiting for someone to respond.

"Hi Robin! This is Tiffany, you contacted me about the Youth Entertainment Assistant job?" A woman said and instinctively I politely sat up straight as if she could see me.

"Oh, yes, hello." I said, unsure of how to proceed.

"Hi!" She repeated, "So I took a look at the resumé you sent me on Facebook, and I'd love to have a chat with you."

I smiled, "Really?"

"Yeah! Can you make a meeting with me tomorrow?" She asked.

Without a moment of hesitation, I agreed. "Yes, yes, I'd love to." I said excitedly.

"Great. Come along to the Community Centre tomorrow at 4:30 before the class, then you can meet the group if you'd like," She said.

"Okay, that sounds great." I told her through a smile. "Thanks so much."

"No problem. See you tomorrow at 4:30." She reiterated.

"Yep, 4:30, see you then." I repeated and heard her hang up. I hadn't noticed but Florence had been sat beside me pressing her ear close to the phone. She had a huge grin on her face, and I'm sure mine matched. We both squealed simultaneously, causing Mom to bolt back into the kitchen.

“What’s going on, what happened, who’s hurt?” She rambled, looking between the two of us. I stood up and practically jumped over to her in excitement. “I got an interview!” I exclaimed.

“Oh, that’s amazing sweetie!” She said, pulling me into a hug. Behind her, I saw Nate sauntering toward the kitchen and leaning against the door frame. “I never thought I’d see you excited about an interview… you’ve been having a tantrum about this all summer.” She added.

To that I heard a snicker from Florence. “This is for a Youth Education Performer Assistant or… something.” I said.

“And what does that mean?” Florence asked.

“The job description said it would be Tuesdays and Thursday nights for 4 hours at the community centre helping out with a children’s tap dancing class.” I explained with a smile on my face as I grabbed one of the sandwiches Mom had made earlier. Finally, I had an appetite.

"That's amazing! Perfect for college applications too!" Florence said and Mom walked up behind me and wrapped her arms around me.

"I'm so proud of you." She said and I hugged her back quickly before munching on the sandwich. I had never tasted anything so wonderful, I guess hangover food was just better than regular food.

"I mean, let's not get ahead of ourselves, it's just an interview." I said. I didn't want to get my mom's hopes up, I didn't even know if I'd get the job or like it. Florence was right though; it would be perfect for my college applications. Even if I did get the job and didn't like it, I'd have to stick it out for that reason alone.

"I didn't know you could tap dance too." Nate said and I turned around to him, still stood in the doorway.

"There's a lot you don't know about me." I replied, catching his eye. After a moment, he left the room and went back to fixing the front door.

I guess it was time to start prepping.

Chapter 16

RobinM110: *I got a job interview!*

MPh2011: *That's great babe. Any news on coming to London?*

Florence and I sat on the roof outside my bedroom window listening to an indie band on Florence's phone as I researched the dance class and Tiffany. She'd gone to my high school, and she'd studied dance in Paris, toured the world and worked on cruise ships then moved back to Fort Collins last year. It's amazing what you can find out from a public Facebook profile.

It was a fairly new dance group, I guess that's why they were hiring. The Facebook page had only been active for a couple of months; there wasn't a website or any information and all I could find was the timetable for the Youth Project on the Community Centre's webpage.

"Okay, my dad said I can stay the night and he'll pick me up at 2pm before we have to go to the airport." Florence said, putting her phone in her pocket and lying back, staring up at the clouds.

"I can't believe you're already leaving." I said sadly as I put my own phone aside and laid down with her. It was slightly cramped up here with two people.

"I know." She said, resting her head on my shoulder. "But when you come to study in New York we can see each other all the time. Hell, we could even live together." She suggested, perking up and sitting straight.

I smiled a little, watching her. "That would be cool." I replied.

"Imagine it! We could get a little loft and make it our own! Two young ladies in New York living our dreams, struggling to make ends meet. You could work in one of those singing cafés while you audition for shows and study and I could be your supportive best friend who writes passive aggressive post-it notes telling you to wash your dishes and decorates the loft so extravagantly that we can barely afford our rent! It would be great!"

As she spoke, I pictured every little detail. I pictured walking through the front door of an apartment, sweaty from a day of rehearsals for whatever show I'd been cast in. I imagined Florence sitting on the couch eating leftover pizza from the delivery we'd got the night before as we stayed up talking until 3am. I thought of video chatting my parents to update them about my week of auditions and rehearsals. It was the dream.

Then I had a sinking feeling. Mason wasn't a part of that dream. Obviously, I hadn't hidden the sad look from my face because Florence turned to me, concern in her eyes. "Is everything okay?" She asked.

I sighed, looking over at Nate's window with his curtain closed. Could Nate be in that dream instead? Or were neither of them even an option? "Am I being an idiot?" I asked plainly.

"What're you talking about?" Florence asked. I tucked my knees into my chest and closed my eyes.

"It's just... everything you just said... it sounds so fun and amazing." I started, "and here I am trying to convince myself that what I really want is to move across the world to live in a country I've never been to with a boy I've never met." I admitted. Florence put her arm around my shoulder and rested her cheek against my head.

"Can you do something for me?" She asked and I looked at her. "Can you for a second forget about Mason, forget about me and your parents, forget about Nate," she started, "and think about you."

I stared at her blankly. "What do you mean?"

"You have to think about what you want to do. You get one life, Boo, don't change your dreams for anyone." She said. I nodded, but I still didn't know what I wanted.

I climbed back into my bedroom. "I'm going to go take a shower." I said, ending the conversation quickly.

"Okay, I'll stay out here if that's okay?" She asked. Munchkin, who I hadn't even noticed was in my room, climbed up and out of the window, perching on Florence's lap. "Oh well, now I can't go anyway. I will stay here until this precious lump leaves." She laughed.

"You realize if you keep giving him attention, he'll never leave." I said with a smile.

"I'm okay with that." She grinned, stroking Munchkin lovingly.

As I came walking back to my room, I tied my damp hair in a high ponytail and watched Munchkin saunter his way down the hallway. I approached my bedroom door and heard Florence's voice from inside talking to someone. Listening through the small open passage that Munchkin had squeezed through, I heard her say "She says she loves him, that's good enough for me".

I raised my eyebrow but stayed stood in the hallway. "I don't think she does." A familiar voice said. It was Nate. Why the hell was he in my room with Florence?

"She's known him for years. People become attached to the people they meet online. If they didn't, I wouldn't be here." She explained. "I love Robin more than anyone, except maybe my dad, and we only met for the first time a few days ago." She explained. I couldn't help but smile a little to myself hearing this. I loved her too.

"I just don't understand it. A friend is one thing, but a relationship?"

"Don't get me wrong, I couldn't be in a relationship with someone I'd met online, but Robin's not like that. She feels things hard. That's why you've been getting in her head so much." Florence explained. I felt my heart drop. She knew me way too well. She'd only been here for a few days and could see perfectly how confused I was about where my life was going, and who was in it.

"I'm in her head?" Nate replied and with that I opened the door and walked in. They both stood up from where they had been sat on my bed and looked guilty.

"Okay, now you guys have had more than enough time to talk, I think it's time you should be heading home." I said abruptly, walking over to Nate and pushing against him, leading him in the direction of the window. Without saying anything, he climbed out the window and looked back at me quickly. When I knew he was definitely back in his own room, I closed the curtain and turned to Florence. "Okay, what the hell?" I asked, a bit more aggressively than I'd intended.

"I'm so sorry, I'd moved over to your bed with Munchkin and before I knew it there was a tap at the window and he was there and he came in and started asking me questions about you and Mason, and I just felt bad for him." Florence defended.

"You felt bad for him?" I asked, "why would you feel bad for him? He's the one that's messing me up."

"You really don't think you're having the same effect on him?" She asked and that caught me off guard. Sure, he'd told me found me attractive. He said he liked being around me and all that stuff, but I'd never thought that I could possibly be causing any kind of problem for him.

"I... guess I never really thought about it." I said, sitting on my bed. She sat down beside me and looked at me sincerely.

"You want my honest advice? I'm kind of on a roll tonight..." She said with a smile and I rolled my eyes.

"I'm going to get it whether I say yes or no, aren't I?" I replied and she grinned.

"You know me so well." She laughed but then her voice got serious. "You need to talk to him. You both need to sit down and discuss what's going on between you. He literally just told me that he can't stop thinking about you,

I know for a fact that you can't stop thinking about him, and I know you're feeling guilty because you're going to be thinking about Mason every time too."

"You seem to be forgetting something." I replied. She just looked at me, waiting for me to continue, "I'm with Mason. I have a boyfriend and I'm committed to him."

"When you go to sleep at night who do you think about? Just be honest." She said. I thought for a second.

"Harry Styles." I said, trying to lighten the mood and move on from the conversation.

"Robin..." She said, pleadingly.

"I... I don't know." I admitted. "I just don't know." I said, and I felt myself wanting to cry. "All I feel lately is guilt. I feel guilty because all I want is to go over to Nate's house and kiss him and be with him and I want Mason to stop blowing up my phone and pressuring me to go to London but I want to meet him because I've spent three years of my life talking to him and I want to know if what I've been experiencing for that long is real or if it's been a waste of time because if it's been a waste of time I just don't know how I'm going to feel because it's felt real this whole time except for when I'm with Nate." I said, taking a breath and letting the tears finally fall. Florence grabbed me into a hug and rubbed my back.

I felt so tired, sad, and relieved all at the same time. I was finally saying everything in my head, and it felt like a weight was lifting.

"Maybe you need to talk to Mason too." Florence suggested, wiping the tears from my cheeks, and smiling at me reassuringly. I nodded.

Suddenly, I heard Mom shout up the stairs telling us that dinner was ready. I took a deep breath, stood up and looked at myself in the mirror. I wiped my eyes, trying to hide the fact that I'd been crying.

I'm so sick of feeling like this.

Chapter 17

MPh2011: *Miss you*

MPh2011: *Can't wait to see you*

MPh2011: *Whenever that is*

"I can't believe you have to go so soon." I said to Florence as we held each other in a tight embrace. Even though I'd had no plans to see her, now that she was here it was like a knife in the heart having to say goodbye. She was the one person in the world that I could literally tell anything to, and I already missed her even though she was stood in front of me.

"I know, it sucks." She replied, still holding me. Munchkin swaggered between my feet and brushed up against both of our legs. "Aw, Munchkin," she said, finally pulling away from me, "I'll see you soon on video chat, I promise!" She exclaimed as she knelt down beside the cat to stroke him one last time.

"I'll come to New York next time." I said. "And soon." I confirmed and she smiled. I saw over her shoulder that her Dad was waiting in his car, tapping the steering wheel impatiently. It was already 2:30pm and Florence was supposed to have left 30 minutes ago.

"Florence," I heard my mom's voice from behind me, "it's been lovely having you here. You're welcome anytime." She said, smiling.

"Thank you, Mrs Montgomery." She said politely and Mom walked away and left us to saying goodbye.

The car horn blasted loudly for the whole cul-de-sac to hear and we knew it was time to officially say goodbye. I grabbed her for one last hug.

"I love you so much," I told her sincerely.

"I love you too, Boo. I'll message you as soon as I get in the car." She told me and I smiled. We were both crying at this point. It was fine saying we'd make sure we saw each other soon, but we both knew that we had no idea when that would be.

Soon enough, she was turning around and walking away from my house. I watched as she climbed into the front seat of her dad's car and continued to stare until they were out of the cul-de-sac and out of sight.

Sniffing, I wiped the tears from my eyes and noticed Nate's grandfather sitting on their porch watching me. He waved at me and I waved back, closing the front door behind me, and walking over.

"Hi Albert." I said, though my croaky voice made it obvious that I'd been crying.

"Good afternoon, Robin." He said with a smile. "Who was that?" He asked.

"Just a friend from New York saying goodbye." I said simply. I doubt his 80-something-year-old mind would be able to comprehend the idea that I was getting this emotional over a friend I'd met on the internet.

"Ah, lovely." He said. He had an old book in his hand, and I glanced down at it. His frail hands stroked the spine and cover carefully and there were pieces of paper sticking out of it in every direction. He clearly noticed me admiring it and held it out in his hand for me to take. "It's one of my diaries, I decided to take a trip down memory lane." He said with a smile. I cautiously took it and sat down beside him on the pristine white bench.

"It's beautiful." I said. "How long have you been writing in it?" I asked, curiously.

"I've had a diary since I was 10. Obviously, this isn't the same one, I've had dozens. This one is from the late 50s, when I got married." He explained and I listened as I flicked through the pages. His writing was hard to read, but I could make out some of it. "My deepest thoughts and feelings recorded in writing since I was a child." He said. "Feels like a lifetime ago..." He paused then laughed, looking down at the diary in my hands, "well, I suppose it was!"

"That's incredible." I said. I turned to one entry that read:

'Today I got married to Annie, the love of my life. She's everything I ever wished a wife would be. She's beautiful, intelligent, and her smile could light up any room she walks into. Though, on this joyous day I cannot help but think of my dear Mai. The fire I felt with her could never

be replaced, and I believe it is important to remember her, especially on a day like today. I love Annie with all my heart, but Mai, you will stay with me forever. My flower, my love, my light.'

I sat there, admiring the words he had written all those years ago and the photo that was stuck beside it of he and his wife on their wedding day. "It's beautiful." I said with a small smile.

"I've always adored writing, and I worry one day, as I get older, my memories will not be what they once were, so looking back on it all one day will be like a brand new adventure." He said, contently. I flipped to another page with a faded photograph of a group of friends. I admired it and saw Albert in the middle holding hands with a girl I assumed to be Annie. Nate was almost identical to his grandfather, it was uncanny. I read the passage alongside it:

'Not a lot happened today. We visited Alan, his wife Betty and their newborn. Little Victor is a very sweet child. I wonder if Annie and I will ever have children. We've been trying, but we've had no luck. Maybe one day.'

I would love to sit down with Albert one day and explore his life. Maybe read more of his journals. It sounded like he'd had an interesting life, maybe even tragic.

I handed him back the dairy as he started to speak. "I gave Geoff a diary when he was a child, but he never took to it." He explained. "When Nate turned 10, I gave him his own diary. He laughed at first, but one evening I went to check on him in bed and he was there scribbling his thoughts into it. I've given him a new diary every year since." Albert smiled. "I'm going to do the same for Jo and Davey when they're older too."

I thought about Nate and about the things he would write about. I wondered if he wrote about Jeremy at all. Maybe he wrote about his friends, or Georgina cheating on him. I thought about the first night he had moved into his house and catching him writing in a journal at 2am as I spied through the window. Selfishly, I wondered if he wrote about me at all.

"That's a really lovely gesture." I said to Albert as I stood up from the bench. "It was good to see you Albert, but I have to go and get ready for a job interview." I told him.

"Oh wonderful! Good luck, my dear." He said with a wide smile and I walked back to my house.

It was 4:15pm when Mom and I arrived at the community centre for my interview. I sat in the car, twiddling my thumbs nervously and checking then double-checking my hair in the sun visor mirror.

"You're going to do great, sweetie." Mom said, patting me on the shoulder reassuringly. "You're more than qualified to teach a group of kids how to tap dance." She said like it was no big deal.

"I'm also more than qualified to be a waitress, and we know how that turned out." I retorted. As I said that, my phone buzzed and I looked down to see what it was, trying to distract myself from my nerves.

Nathaniel Lewis: *Good luck today, you'll be great.*

I stared at the Facebook message for what felt like forever, biting my bottom lip, and smiling. It was a sweet gesture. I thought about whether to reply when he sent another message.

Nathaniel Lewis: *Try not to trip over any children.*

I laughed as I read it and shook my head, putting my phone in my small backpack along with my tap shoes, just in case I was asked to dance. It was my mom's idea; I never would have thought of it otherwise.

"Okay, honey, I love you, but you're going to be late if you don't get out now and I want to go shopping before everything closes." Mom explained and I shook my head.

"Okay, okay, fine, I got this." I said, attempting to hype myself up but it didn't work. Eventually, I climbed out of the car and made my way to the front entrance of the community centre.

An older woman sat there with her glasses on the tip of her nose and a string attached to them hanging around her neck. She looked like every librarian I had ever seen in any movie.

"Hi..." I said shyly. "I'm here to see Tiffany Offpen." I stated, and she looked up at me for the first time.

"To the right, down the hall, past the girl's bathroom. Room 11." She explained, then went back to concentrating on her computer screen, which from the reflection in her glasses I could see was a game of Candy Crush.

"Thank you." I said, gripping the strap of my bag tightly as I walked. I clenched my fists hard, trying to get rid of any excess adrenaline that was going to make me a nervous wreck during this. I quickly grabbed my phone from my bag and looked at the time. I still had 5 minutes before the interview.

Without thinking, I turned into the girl's bathroom and stared at myself in the mirror. "Okay, you got this." I said. I looked at myself, and wished I'd gone for a dress with a higher neckline, and a blazer that didn't make me sweat buckets, and heels instead of flats to make myself look more sophisticated. I shook my head, there was nothing I could do now.

I left the bathroom and headed to the room. The door had a small window, and I took a peek. Inside, there was the woman I'd seen in all the photos on Facebook dancing on cruises and across the world. She was heaving what looked like a heavy box across the room. I slowly creaked the door open and made my way in.

Tiffany turned and looked at me with a smile. "Hi!" She said, placing the box down on the ground and walking over to me. Every footstep echoed from her tap shoes hitting the hardwood floor.

"Hello." I said, clearly nervous. "I'm Robin." I added.

"Yes, hi, I'm Tiffany. It's good to meet you." She replied with a smile. "Sorry it's a mess in here." She said and I looked around to a small, distinctly not-messy room. All that was in here was her bag, sweater, and sneakers in the corner on the floor, a few stacks of plastic bright orange chairs and a couple of boxes of what looked like children's tap shoes and costumes. "Grab a chair." She said and I followed her lead, doing just that.

"Okay, so, I was very impressed with your resumé, Robin. How long have you been dancing again?" She asked.

"Um... well, as long as I can remember really. I've done ballet, tap, contemporary, hip hop, all sorts." I explained.

"That's great. And you're going into your senior year this fall, yes?" She said, crossing her legs elegantly and leaning back in her chair. I sat there straight backed, clearly not relaxed in any way.

"Yes, yes, that's correct." I said.

"Well, the classes will be running all year, so do you think you could handle that after school twice a week? Obviously, we'd give you time off if you had exams or college interviews but generally, you think you'd be able to do it?" She asked.

"Yes, yes, definitely." I agreed.

"Wonderful." She said with a smile. "So, where do you see yourself in five years?"

I paused. I barely knew where I saw myself in the next few months, let alone in five years. How was I supposed to say 'I don't know because I'm in love with a boy from England who wants me to move there but I think I'm also falling for a boy here but I want to dance in New York too with my best friend, so I have no clue' to a complete stranger?

"Um..." I started. "I guess, hopefully working in musical theater, dancing mostly, having graduated college, with an agent and stuff." I said, trying to be a vague as possible.

"Ah, a musical theater girl." She said with a smile. "Well, hopefully this will be a step toward that." She stated. "How're you with kids?" She moved on and I breathed a sigh of relief.

"Depends on the kid." I joked and I heard her laugh a little. "I like children, I think I'm good with them." I admitted. "Though, I'm an only child and haven't had much experience around kids."

"That's fine. The children in this class are a nice bunch so you shouldn't have a problem." She said as she stood up from her chair. "Now enough of this boring professional stuff, what size feet are you? Let's have a quick dance." She said and I stood up with her.

"I actually brought my tap shoes, so don't worry about that." I told her.

"Oh, you come prepared, I like that." She said. Mentally, I thanked Mom for making me bring them. I smiled at her then placed my blazer and bag on the floor beside her own and grabbed my tap shoes. I slipped off my flats and put them on quickly.

For the next 15 minutes, Tiffany and I had fun dancing and tapping away to a tune from Singing in the Rain. I liked her. She seemed impressed with me, and I did some of the flashier moves that I could muster to try and score some points with her.

Eventually, we had to stop, when the first child in the group arrived with her mother. They walked in and Tiffany paused the music in the middle of our rough routine. "Hello Jasmine." She said to the little blonde girl.

"Hi!" Jasmine replied. She must have been about Nate's sister's age. Her Mom grabbed the two of them some chairs and they sat down at the side of the room. Soon enough, more parents and children started arriving and I started to feel a little out of place. I didn't know whether to stay or leave, so I shuffled back to where I'd put my bag and stood there awkwardly, waiting for some sort of direction from Tiffany.

After a few minutes, a group of about 8 students, 7 girls and 1 boy, were sat on the floor ready for class to start. Tiffany clapped her hands loudly and they all stopped talking, looking at their teacher eagerly.

"Okay class, I have someone I'd like you to meet today." She said and I looked around to see if anyone important-looking was in the room. There were only parents. "This is Robin," she said, gesturing for me to walk forward toward the group, "she's our new assistant. She's going to be helping you guys every week!" and the class all looked at me.

I couldn't fight the smile from my face. "Wait, really?" I asked, suddenly very aware that I was stood in front of the class. Tiffany laughed and nodded.

"Everyone, go grab a pair of shoes!" She said, clapping her hands again before leading me over to the side of the room.

"It doesn't pay much, only minimum wage, but I think you'll be a great fit." She told me and I grinned widely.

“Thank you so much!” I replied. “I wish I could stay for the class but honestly I didn’t expect to get the job and my mom’s outside waiting in the car.” I explained.

Tiffany simply laughed. “That’s okay. See you on Tuesday, yeah? Maybe come a bit earlier than 5pm so we can keep working on that routine.” She suggested and I nodded enthusiastically.

“Thank you again!” I said then turned to the class. They all looked so sweet putting on their tap shoes. “I’ll see you guys next week!” I said to them and some of them waved goodbye while others flat-out ignored me, but nothing could bring me down right now.

I walked out the room and left for the exit, completely forgetting I was still wearing my tap shoes and my footsteps were echoing through the corridor. I speed-walked outside and grabbed my phone from my bag.

Without thinking, I unlocked it, opened my Facebook chat with Nate and pressed the call button. I sat down on the steps outside and started fumbling to change my shoes while I pressed the phone to my ear with my shoulder.

“Hello?” I heard him say.

"I got the job!" I exclaimed excitedly. "I got the fucking job!" I repeated and I heard him laugh.

"Congrats, little lady." He said, and I was still grinning from ear to ear.

"You're now talking to the Youth Entertainment Assistant for Tiffany's Dance and Performance Youth Project." I said.

"That's a mouthful." He said and we both laughed.

"Regardless, that's my title now, you must kneel before me as I reign over these little kids in their tap shoes." I joked and I heard him laugh.

"You're so weird." He snickered.

"I can almost hear you smirking down the phone." I commented. I was full of so much confidence right now it was almost out of character.

"So, what're you doing now?" He asked and I looked around at the street.

"Currently I'm trying to change out of my tap shoes on the front steps of the community centre while I wait for Mom to pick me up, but she's shopping so God only knows when that's going to be." I explained.

"Well, if you need a ride home, I'm just finishing work myself, so I can come and get you if you want." He suggested and I felt butterflies in my stomach.

"That would be ideal." I replied, "I'll text my mom and tell her so she doesn't think I've been abducted or anything."

"Probably for the best." He said. "Okay, I'll see you in a few minutes."

"Okay, see you." I replied, then the phone line went dead.

As I sat there, texting Mom, I realised what I had done. Why had my first instinct, before anything else, before I'd even changed my shoes, been to call Nate? Why hadn't I called Mason? Or Florence? Or even Mom? Nate was the first person I wanted to tell, and frankly the only person.

"That's amazing sweetie, I'm so proud of you! We'll get take-out tonight to celebrate! What do you want? Pizza?" Mom asked excitedly on the other end of the phone. "I'm just grabbing some frozen yoghurt and I'll head right over to pick you up; I'll get you some strawberry yoghurt too." She said and I could almost hear her grinning.

"Oh, don't worry about that." I told her. "Actually, Nate's coming to pick me up." I admitted. "He just finished work and offered me a lift back with him, it's no big deal."

"I didn't say it was." She said. "Invite him round for dinner, we'll all celebrate. Your Dad should be back home in a couple of hours." There was another pause. "Now honey, I have to ask..." She started and I felt my body tense slightly. "You and Nate, you're... well, you know, with Mason and everything, and how much you've been wanting to meet him, I just want to make sure you're-"

"We're just friends, Mom." I told her bluntly, even if I didn't quite believe it when I said it. Mom could see right through my lies normally, I couldn't imagine what she was thinking right now.

"Okay, okay." She said. "Now, don't be home too late."

"We're coming straight home; I'll probably be there before you." I told her, walking to the edge of the sidewalk and looking down the road to see if I could spot Nate in his car. No sign of him yet.

“Okay, I’ll see you soon, love you.”

“Love you too.” I said and hung up the phone. With no sign of Nate yet, I quickly made my way back into the Community Centre and down the hall to the girl’s bathroom. I looked at myself in the mirror again, now still as nervous as I was the last time I was here, but for a completely different reason.

I toyed with the idea of putting my blazer back on so that I wasn’t as exposed in just a dress around Nate, but it was far too hot outside and I’d rather have him exposed to my bare arms (God forbid!) than be sweating buckets in his car.

I continued to stare at myself, grabbing a hair tie from my wrist and placing my hair in a high ponytail which somehow still managed to make my hair reach nearly the middle of my back. For a brief second, as I stared at my sandy blonde hair, I wondered if Nate preferred brunettes. Not that it mattered.

I wiped what was once pristine eyeliner from my eyes, attempting to make myself look like a presentable human then took a deep breath.

"What're you doing?" I asked myself. "He's not going to care if your eyeliner is wonky, or if you wear a blazer or not, or if your hair is tied up. You shouldn't even care. You have a boyfriend. You idiot." I said. Suddenly, I heard a toilet flush behind me, and I felt my entire face burn red.

A little girl came walking out cautiously, looking at me. She was wearing a blue leotard, a flowing green skirt and tap shoes and I mentally slapped myself. "Hi Miss Robin." She said, reaching awkwardly to wash her hands beside me.

"Hello." I said, trying to pretend she hadn't just caught me talking to myself. "What's your name?" I asked.

"I'm Izzy" She said. She sounded so innocent and sweet. My heart melted.

"Nice to meet you Izzy, I'll be back for class next week." I explained, passing her a paper towel to dry her hands.

“Miss Robin...” She said, looking up at me. I bent down to her height and listened, “is your boyfriend nice?”

I smiled weakly. “He’s lovely.” I told her. “He’s British.” I added.

“Is the other boy British?” She asked and I shook my head. “Is he nice?”

“He’s...” I paused. “He’s...” My heart started to ache again. “Yes, he’s nice.” I said simply. “Now go on, head back to class, Miss Offpen is probably waiting for you.” I said and Izzy smiled at me then tapped her way out of the bathroom.

I checked my phone and saw a missed call from Nate. I pulled myself together, took one last look in the mirror and headed out. He was parked outside, and I could see him checking himself out in his rear view mirror and fixing his hair. He quickly stopped when he spotted me and honked the horn three times loudly. I laughed and walked round to the passenger side, climbing in.

“Thanks for the ride.” I said, trying desperately to hide the smile from my face and failing miserably.

"No problem, little lady." He said and I rolled my eyes. "Congratulations on the job. Hope you didn't trip over any of the children." He joked.

"I didn't, but one did just catch me in the bathroom talking to myself in the mirror." I admitted with a small laugh and he laughed too.

"Why were you talking to yourself?" He said as he started the car and began to drive.

I hesitated, "I'm clearly just psychotic." I snickered and I caught him roll his eyes. He was smiling too, almost as much as I seemed to be. I couldn't help it, I liked being around him, he made me feel like a little girl with a crush on a celebrity. Wait, did I just admit I have a crush on him? I shook the thought away and looked out at the road.

"This isn't the way home..." I said as I noticed he was driving in the complete opposite direction.

"Yeah, about that, I've decided to kidnap you." He said and I turned to him abruptly.

"Sorry, what?" I asked.

"I figured we could celebrate the fact that you didn't fuck up your interview by doing something fun." He said.

I thought for a moment. It wasn't necessarily a bad idea.

"What did you have in mind?" I asked.

"I thought maybe we could go to the reservoir?" He suggested. It wasn't exactly what I was expecting, but then again, I didn't know what I was expecting. I wouldn't necessarily call the reservoir fun though.

"Um... sure, I guess." I said and for some reason the air between us seemed to thicken, like there was a tension neither of us wanted to acknowledge. I stared forward, watching as we drove through downtown and toward the exit to the reservoir.

I hadn't been there for years, I used to go with my parents, we'd take a picnic and I'd skim stones with Dad. Then he got made a senior associate, his schedule became so much busier and the picnics just stopped. I didn't mind though, I was growing up, and I didn't have much of an interest in family picnics after a while.

We both sat in silence for most of the ride, thankfully it was a relatively short drive, but something was definitely still hanging between us. I was thinking about what I'd heard him talking about the night before with Florence, the things he'd said to me the night after our families went for dinner, the words he could have been writing in his journal. Not once did I think of Mason.

Until my phone rang, and I saw his name flashing on the screen. I noticed Nate take a look at the screen too, and his hands tensed around the steering wheel. I thought for a second, then decided I'd better pick up.

"Hi..." I said, quietly.

"Hi, how'd the interview go?" He asked immediately.

"Oh, I got the job." I said, a lot more solemnly than I had earlier when I called Nate.

"That's amazing, I knew you could do it." He said. I listened to his voice, his accent which a few weeks ago would have made me melt just hearing it, now just made me feel... well... not a lot.

"Thanks," I said, "I'm celebrating with my family and... a friend, tonight, so I probably won't be around to talk." I said. I forced myself not to look at Nate as I spoke, keeping my gaze on the road ahead.

"That's okay, I'm heading to bed in a minute anyway, I just thought I'd call and check up on you." He said.

"Listen, I know things have been a bit weird between us lately, I just wanted to say sorry."

At this, I felt my heart flutter a little. Hearing him admit to what had been going on, knowing that he felt just as strange about the situation as I did, it felt like a weight was almost lifting.

"That's okay..." I said. "Listen, I've gotta go, but I'll talk to you tomorrow."

"Okay, I love you." Mason said and I hesitated.

"Yeah, you too." I said. I didn't want to say those words right now. Not with Nate sitting right beside me, not when I wasn't sure I was even feeling them.

Chapter 18

***RobinM110** — No new messages.*

The rest of the drive was silent, and as we pulled up to a small parking lot by the reservoir, I felt like getting a ride with Nate and spending the evening with him maybe wasn't the best idea after all.

"So..." He said as we just sat there awkwardly, or at least, I felt awkward.

"So..." I repeated. A few moments past, and he climbed out the car and I followed suit, deciding to leave my bag, blazer, and phone in the front seat.

We began walking together and I looked out at the sun reflecting off the water. It was a hot day, but not unbearably so. Glancing over at Nate, I noticed he was still wearing his Kingfisher t-shirt and I could smell the remnants of seafood and dish soap. A weird mix, but I kind of liked it.

“Can I ask you something?” Nate said eventually. He stopped by the water and grabbed a small rock from the ground, staring at it, and he threw it hard. It went so far; I barely saw it until I noticed the small splash where it hit the water.

“Why did you call me after your interview?”

It’s not what I was expecting, but it was a big question, nonetheless. “I, um...” I began, not sure what I was even saying. I walked up next to him and picked up a stone, skimming it across the water almost effortlessly and I could feel his eyes on me. I ignored it, picked up another stone, and skimmed it. “I don’t know.” I admitted. It was the truth. He didn’t respond, and I felt the need to keep talking. “It was sort of... a reflex. Maybe because you messaged me just before I went in, so you were on my mind.” I explained.

“That’s why I was on your mind?” He said, grabbing a rock and following my lead, attempting to skim a rock but failing.

"Well, yeah." I said. It wasn't a lie necessarily, just not the whole truth. We stood in silence for a few minutes, skimming stones and looking out at the lake, occasionally stealing glances at each other. "I spoke to Albert today." I said.

He raised his eyebrow at me. "You spoke to my Poppa?" He asked. I smiled a little.

"Yeah. He was sitting on your porch earlier when I was saying bye to Florence." I explained. "He had this diary with him. He let me read it." I paused before adding, "he told me you write diaries too."

He tossed a larger rock high into the air, and we both watched it splash, rippling the water toward us and I looked down at my reflection in the surface then looked at Nate's beside me. "I wouldn't call them diaries... bit girly." He said and I rolled my eyes.

"It's not girly to keep a record of your thoughts. Albert's was beautiful. I read about his wedding day, and the woman he fell in love with during the Vietnam war. The one he said wanted to be a performer like me." I said. "I don't know how he knew that though." I shrugged, taking a seat on the ground, adjusting myself on the rocks and slipping my feet out of my flats and dipping them into the water. The cold shivered through me, but eventually I got used to the feeling.

Nate sat down beside me, so close that if I moved even an inch to the right we would be touching. “I told him.” He said. I expected as much.

“How come?” I asked, curiously.

He simply shrugged. “He asked what I was writing about in my journal. I told him I was writing about this girl who was driving me insane, but I couldn’t stop thinking about her, and then he started asking me questions.” I was now hanging on his every word but continued to stare down at the water. I felt my breath catch in my throat. I wanted to hear more, I wanted so desperately for him to keep talking.

“I told him your name, that you were a really good dancer and that your window is right across from mine which makes it hard to stop thinking about you, especially when I see you sitting there on your phone or singing musical songs that you think I can't hear even though I definitely can and it's the reason I keep my window open,"

I could feel myself blushing now, and the butterflies in my stomach were going crazy. Suddenly, no one existed except the two of us. Mason was no one, Georgina was no one. It was just us.

"That's when my mom told us we were going for dinner that night with your family and I immediately regretted saying anything because I know that Poppa can't keep a secret to save his life and I knew you were angry at me that day, so I definitely didn't want him saying anything." He snickered a little to himself. "Not that it matters now I've told you."

Suddenly, I felt him move closer to me, and our sides were touching. His leg brushed softly against mine and I felt the tips of his fingers slightly touch my own hand. I felt myself practically stop breathing and realised that this was the thing I'd seen in movies. When people talk about electricity or sparks or whatever it was, this was that moment.

"I'm sorry I talked to your friend about you last night, by the way." He started and I shook my head.

"It's okay." I told him. I turned and looked at him for the first time since we sat down. He was staring at me and my head was spinning at a thousand miles an hour, my heart was pounding like crazy, and I was feeling so many things that I didn't even know what to focus on.

We sat there together, silently, looking into each other's eyes when I felt Nate reach his hand up and brush his fingers against my cheek. I felt a shiver course through me, and my breath hitched in my throat. He held his palm against my cheek, and I felt myself close my eyes, almost instinctively. I breathed in his scent, the smell of soap from his hand and too-strong-deodorant in the slow summer breeze.

That's when it happened. A moment I hadn't even known I'd been waiting for. His lips brushed against mine and I felt myself kiss him back. It was soft and slow. It was nothing I'd ever imagined Nate could be. I pressed my lips against his harder, and he reciprocated instantly. His hand moved down to the side of my neck and I felt him move closer to me. The kiss grew deeper and hungrier, and I reached up and rested my hand against his bicep. I never would have thought my first kiss would be with Nathaniel Lewis and not Mason.

Wait... Mason...

I pulled away slowly, and he rested his forehead against mine. I kept my eyes closed for a second then opened them, seeing him looking at me with his beautiful eyes.

"Hi..." He said, almost breathlessly. He was smiling wide and I imagined I looked the same. The butterflies started to subside though, and the guilt was making its way back.

"You have no idea how long I've wanted to do that." He said. We continued to stare at each other, practically in a trance.

"Me too." I admitted. He leaned forward again, and his lips pressed against mine, but I pulled away. "I can't though..." I told him sadly. He looked upset and moved away from me slightly. "I meant what I said about Mason, I can't give up on him before I've even met him."

Nate pushed himself off the ground, not saying anything, and I slipped my feet out of the water and back into my shoes. He held his hand out and helped me up. "We should go." He stated, avoiding eye contact with me.

"Yeah..." I agreed.

Now what was I supposed to do?

I sat with my parents at the dinner table, picking at my Chinese food with a pair of cheap chopsticks. "Honey, you look sad." Dad said after we'd all sat in silence for uncomfortably long. "We thought you'd be really excited to start a job, especially a dance job." He added.

I simply shrugged. "I am excited, really." I told them. I was, I just couldn't focus on that right now. I kept getting flashbacks to the kiss. The way Nate's hand felt against my neck, how soft his lips were, how desperately I wanted to kiss him again. My stomach was turning just at the thought of it. I snapped out of it and noticed my parents both staring at me as I barely ate.

"Honestly." I said, trying to reassure them. "I met the class and the kids were sweet, Tiffany is really nice too, we started choreographing a little routine together before class started. It was fun." I said.

"Well, your Mom and I are incredibly proud of you." Dad said and I smiled weakly at them, fumbling with some noodles. Defeated, I tossed my chopsticks to the side and grabbed a fork.

"So proud, in fact, that we got you something to celebrate." Mom added and my ears perked up. I looked between the two of them and Mom had a huge grin on her face. It was almost suspicious.

"What's going on?" I asked, cautiously. Mom stood up from the table and grabbed something from the kitchen counter nearby, an envelope, then handed it over to me. I took it and stared at it. It was just plain white envelope with my name scrawled across the front.

"Go on, open it." Dad said and I peeled the envelope open and grabbed the paper from inside. Unfolding them, I read it, confused.

My eyes widened and I looked between Mom and Dad again. "Are you joking?" I said, in disbelief. In my hand I was holding two plane tickets from Denver to London for next weekend. “You’re joking, right?” I repeated.

“Nope, completely real.” Mom said and I stared at the tickets. “Your Dad can’t come because of work, but we’re leaving early Friday morning, it’s a 12-hour flight, so we’ll be there late, but we’ll have Saturday and Sunday.”

“I can’t believe this.” I admitted. “I don’t even know what to say.”

“Maybe a thank you?” Dad said and I smiled, standing up and heading over to Mom, giving her a hug, then Dad.

“Can I go and call Mason?” I asked and Dad rolled his eyes.

“Of course.” He said and I ran out of the kitchen, upstairs and into my room where Munchkin was snoring loudly on my bed. I sat down beside him, scratching him under the chin, causing him to stretch against me and let out a huge yawn. Checking the time, I realised Mason was probably still asleep, but I decided to try calling him anyway.

I listened to the phone ring for a couple of minutes before hanging up. I could just tell him in the morning.

Next, I decided to call Florence. I had to talk to her about the day. She'd been messaging me all day on her way home, but I hadn't had a chance to respond.

"Hey Boo!" She said and I smiled at the sound of her voice.

"Hey," I said, my voice tired. I stared out my window as I talked. Nate's curtain was closed. "How was your flight?" I asked.

"Boring. They didn't have any good movies." She said. "I ended up just watching some weird show on Amazon Prime about people that live in virtual reality." She explained.

"I kissed Nate." I blurted out.

"You WHAT?" She said, practically screeching down the phone. "Tell me *everything*!"

"And I'm going to London next week. My parents bought me tickets because I got the job."

"Woah, what a day." She said. "Okay, first things first, you got the job! I'm so proud of you!"

"Thanks," I said, smiling a little.

"Next: London! That's good, you'll get to finally meet Mason, you'll get to see if everything's real and if you do want to study there. It'll definitely help you make a decision and figure out what the heck is going on." She explained. "Last thing: Nate! How, when, why, how and *how*?" She asked eagerly. I couldn't help but laugh a little.

"Well... I mean, I got the job and I called him to tell him and-"

"I'm going to stop you there, you called him instead of me and I'm offended, but continue." She joked and I shook my head.

"Okay, sorry. Anyway, I called him, he picked me up from the community centre, we went up to the reservoir to celebrate-"

"Ooooh the 'reservoir', sounds sexy."

I couldn't help but laugh. "Do you want me to tell you or not?"

"Sorry, continue."

"Okay so, we were at the reservoir, we were skimming rocks, and he was telling me that he talked to his grandfather about me, and he was just being very sweet and I don't know, one thing led to another and before I know it he's kissing me and I'm kissing him back and I just lost myself." I rambled. "Then I started thinking about Mason, and I felt bad and pulled away."

Florence sighed down the phone. "I'm sorry, Robin." She said. "It must suck not to be able to be with the person you really want to be with."

"Next week, when I see Mason, I'll know for sure." I told her. I heard someone calling Florence's name on the other end of the phone.

"I'm sorry Boo, I have to go, but I'll message you later. I love you".

"I love you too." I replied and she hung up.

Chapter 19

RobinM110: *Couldn't get hold of you, but figured you'd wake up and see this.*

RobinM110: *My Mom bought us plane tickets to London for next week! We're finally going to meet!*

I stared up at the ceiling wide-eyed. I couldn't sleep, no matter how hard I tried. I took a glimpse at my alarm clock: 1:30am. This was going to be a long night.

I climbed out of bed, shuffling my feet into my slippers shaped like Mickey Mouse and left my room, quietly sneaking down the stairs. I could hear Dad snoring loudly from my parent's bedroom down the hall–how Mom managed to fall asleep next to him every night baffled me. As I walked down the stairs, I looked at photographs of my parents and I through the years that lined the stairway. Pictures of us at Disney World, a photo of me graduating from Kindergarten, my parents on their wedding day and one school picture Dad decided to frame as a joke because I had blood on my chin. I was late for picture day because I'd had a dentist appointment that morning. Mom tried to rush me to the school in time, and we made it, but my mouth was numb from having a tooth extracted and I'd bled down my chin and no one had said anything. I didn't know until I went to the bathroom about an hour later. It was humiliating.

I trudged my way to the kitchen and opened the refrigerator, the light blinding me for a second. I grabbed a carton of orange juice and poured myself a glass, sitting down at the counter and sighing. My thoughts just wouldn't stop. All I wanted was to sleep and feel good because I got a job that was fun and that could help me with my college applications. But here I was, restless and wide awake because all I was thinking about was Nate and Mason.

Am I a bad person? I kissed a guy who's not my boyfriend, that pretty much makes me one of the worst kinds of people, right? But does it count if I haven't even met said boyfriend? Of course it counts, he's been in my heart and my life for three years, it's not like it never meant anything. Mason was- no, *is* my first love.

As my thoughts went round and round in my head, I spotted a figure out the window in Nate's garden. Cautiously, I stood up and spied outside. It was his little sister, sitting in the moonlight with a telescope. I smiled and took a stroll out to my garden and peered over the fence. Just then, I noticed Geoff was sat in a lawn chair with a can of beer and a book. Sensing my presence, he looked directly at me, startled.

"Jesus Christ, Robin!" He exclaimed, standing up and walking toward me.

"Oh my God, I'm so sorry." I apologised profusely.

"Why are you wandering the garden at this hour?" He asked, and I took a glance over at Jo, who was still minding her own business with a telescope.

"Couldn't sleep." I admitted. "What's going on here?" I asked.

"I'm looking at the stars and planets." Jo called over to me.

"Shhh, Jo, it's late, don't shout." Geoff hushed her. "She likes to look at the planets, so we have to plan our nights accordingly. She napped earlier, so she could stay up late and see Jupiter tonight." He explained.

"That's really cool." I said with a small smile. The stars were bright tonight, so I imagine Jo was having a good time.

"Do you want to come and look?" Jo said in a loud whisper.

I hesitated. "Uh, yeah sure." I agreed.

"Come on over." Geoff said with a smile. I thought about walking around, then decided to jump the fence. I heaved myself up and over and landed relatively gracefully on the grass on the other side. "Impressive." Geoff commented and I laughed a little.

I walked over to Jo and she was sat on a blanket, scribbling some notes down roughly in a small notebook. "This is really cool." I said, gesturing to the telescope.

"I know." She said and I smiled, sitting down beside her on the blanket.

“So, you like astronomy then?” I asked the girl. Her hair was tied up in a loose bun and she wore pink and yellow spotted pyjamas.

“Yeah.” She said. “I look up at the sky to see Jeremy.” She commented and I was a little taken aback.

Geoff walked up beside us and sat down next to Jo. “Jeremy was-”

“I know,” I interrupted, “Sorry...” I said. “Nate told me.” I explained.

Geoff nodded simply. “Ah, of course he did.” He said. He looked at me with a small smile. “He trusts you a lot.”

I felt the butterflies in my stomach again. “Nate named a star after him for me.” Jo said and I felt my heart melt. Nate was so much more than I ever thought he could be. He was sweet and kind and more caring than I could have ever possibly imagined. I always thought he was such an awful person just because he was “popular”, how wrong I was.

“Where’s Jeremy in the sky then?” I asked and Jo shot up from the blanket and looked through the telescope, positioning it, looking at a chart occasionally as she did so.

Eventually, she gestured for me to stand up and I did, leaning down and looking through the telescope. Through the scope I saw a shining star, brighter than the rest around it. I'm sure there was some science, some interesting facts about it–maybe where it was in the sky or why it was seemingly brighter than the rest, but I didn't know anything about astronomy and I wasn't about to start guessing.

"That's amazing." I said. "He's beautiful." I told her sincerely. I moved away from the telescope, and she began to look through it again. "Do you mind if I go and get myself some water?" I asked and Geoff nodded.

"Be my guest." He said and I heard Jo begin to hum the same song from Beauty and the Beast under her breath. This was a girl after my own heart.

I walked through the house and it was so different to the last time I was here. The painted walls were complete, there weren't any boxes strewn around and the furniture was no longer plastic-wrapped. As I poured myself a glass of water from the faucet, I sighed and heard a creak behind me. I turned abruptly.

“Um... hi...” Nate said, staring at me, clearly incredibly confused. I stared at him standing there and glanced down seeing his shirtless body highlighted by the moonlight through the window. There he was abs fully on show with a pair of baggy striped pyjama pants. Suddenly, all my thoughts jumbled, and I forgot how to breathe. I gulped nervously. How did one guy look so perfect?

“Oh Jesus, sorry, I um... yeah... I should go.” I said, fumbling with my glass, placing it on the counter.

“Not before you tell me why you’re in my house at nearly 2am.” Nate said quickly, and I felt the blood rush to my face. Right now, I was desperate to be back in my own room, in my bed, away from here.

“I um... I couldn’t sleep.” I said, as if that explained it.

“So, you, what? Broke into my house?” He asked. I wanted a trapdoor to open up below me and I didn’t care what was under it, whatever it was would have been better than here.

“God, no, um... I was in my garden and your Dad and sister were out looking at stars and stuff and they invited me to look and so I did and- it’s really sweet that you named a star after your brother for Jo, really- and I um, I just wanted a glass of water and I- Jesus, sorry, I'll just go." I rambled.

I hadn't even noticed that he had been moving closer to me and now I wished I was wearing more than simply a tank top, pyjama shorts and Mickey Mouse slippers, because I could feel his gaze trailing down me.

"Calm down." He laughed, and he reached behind me, practically pressing our bodies together, and grabbed my abandoned glass of water. We stood there together, inches away from one another and I felt my back pressed up against the counter behind me.

"Robin is everything oka-" I heard, and we both turned to see Geoff standing there staring at us. "Okaaaay then." He said, holding his hands up and backing out of the room. "As you were." He snickered.

"Jesus Christ," Nate said, shaking his head as we watched his father leave. He backed away from me slowly and I couldn't stop myself from flicking my gaze down at his body. Everything about him seemed so effortless. His hair was messy like he'd just woken up, but stylishly so, and his chest and abs were just... wow. “Listen, I’m um... I’m sorry about earlier.” He said in a hushed voice, I guessed so that he didn’t wake his Mom or little brother.

“Don’t be.” I said before thinking. At this, he seemed to breathe a sigh.

“Good, because I’m not really sorry.” He said with a smirk. The same smirk I’d seen so many times. The one that made me melt. We stood staring at each other for a few seconds.

“My mom’s taking me to London next week.” I told him suddenly and I felt him retreat from me. “I’m sorry.” I said then without a second thought I rushed past him, feeling our skin brush briefly, and hurried out the front door and to my own house.

Chapter 20

MPh2011: *I can't believe this is finally happening.*

RobinM110: *Me too. Three years in the making.*

MPh2011: *Let me know when you arrive!*

The week that followed went by surprisingly quickly. I had managed to get through two work shifts without messing up, Jason's dance for the agent went well and I hadn't bumped into Nate or spoken to him once. We'd spied each other through our windows every once in a while, but that was all. I managed to finally put my attention back on Mason, and that was desperately needed in the build up to seeing him.

"And you've definitely got everything?" Dad asked Mom as we stood at the front door. It was 2am, I was tired, and I was not ready to spend 12 hours straight on a plane.

"Yes," Mom reassured him, "it's only a couple of days, we're good." She said, leaning in and kissing him on the cheek. As they said their goodbyes, I walked over to the cab which was waiting for us at the end of the driveway. I placed my suitcase in the trunk of the car and turned around, looking over at my parents. I saw them kiss and I sighed, they always made love look so easy.

In the corner of my eye, I saw a curtain move at the window of Nate's lounge. I spotted him standing there, staring at me. How did he know we were leaving at this time? We weren't being loud, it's not like we could have woken him up. I watched him longingly and decided against my better judgement to give him a small wave. He waved back, closed the curtain, and he was gone.

Mom approached me, placing her bag in the trunk next to mine, and we both climbed in the back seat. Soon enough, we were on our way to Denver and I could already feel myself falling asleep as we drove.

Before I knew it, Mom was shaking me awake. I looked out the window, yawning and feeling a bit dazed, and saw

Denver International Airport lit up in front of me. It was far too bright for this time in the morning.

I climbed out of the car as Mom paid the cab driver the fare and clicked my phone screen on. It was just past 3am and our flight was in an hour and a half. Quickly, I snapped a photo of the outside of the airport and sent it to Mason.

RobinM110: *It's happening [image attached]*

He responded almost instantly.

MPh2011: *Not long now*

I slipped my phone back into my pocket and followed Mom into the airport to check in. It was eerily quiet, and I stuck to Mom close. At times like these, in unfamiliar surroundings, I felt like a child. It made me wonder how I'd ever deal with moving away from home–but that's a problem for future Robin. Right now, I had to focus on two things: Mason, and keeping my eyes open.

I fell asleep again as we waited to board the plane, but before I knew it, I was sat beside an airplane window, looking out at the runway and wanting nothing more than to go back to sleep.

"Try not to sleep too much during the flight Robin." Mom said and I nodded while yawning. "We'll arrive at about midnight their time so if we stay awake and sleep when we get there, we won't get hit so bad with jet lag." She explained as I felt my head drooping and my whole body seemingly wanting to force me into a coma.

"Mmhmm" I replied with my eyes closed and before the plane even took off, I was asleep again.

When I woke up, the sky was a bright blue out the window, and I squinted as I adjusted to the light. I had absolutely no idea what time it was. I stretched as much as I could in my cramped plane seat and turned around to Mom, who had put a blanket over me while I was sleeping. She was eating what looked like a croissant while flipping through the in-flight channels.

"Morning sleepyhead." She said, handing me a croissant wrapped in a napkin. I took it as I rubbed my eyes.

“Morning.” I replied.

“I got a Wi-Fi package so you can let Mason know how the flight is going.” She said and I tiredly pulled my phone out from my bag and connected to the Wi-Fi with the information Mom read out to me from a small slip of paper.

As it connected, my phone immediately started to buzz, almost non-stop.

“Wow, you’re popular.” Mom commented and I rolled my eyes. When I saw what it was, my heart dropped. A stream of messages from Nathaniel, sent a couple of hours after I’d left.

Nathaniel Lewis: *I hate that you’re going to meet this guy. You shouldn't be with him and you know it. I’ve never felt anything like I have with you and I know you probably think I’m being stupid, and that you have to give this guy a try, but if you really loved him then none of this stuff between us would have happened.*

Nathaniel Lewis: *I know I shouldn’t even be saying this, but I can’t get you out of my head. I can barely sleep* *or eat or focus on anything because no matter what, my brain keeps going back to you.*

Nathaniel Lewis: *I wish I could have stopped you from going, and I know that no matter what I tell you now it's going to be too late because you're already going, but I don't want to give up so easy.*

Nathaniel Lewis: *I won't give up so easy.*

Nathaniel Lewis: *You're like... one of the best people I've ever met. You're passionate and you're beautiful and you're funny and you just get me.*

Nathaniel Lewis: *I know I shouldn't have kissed you that day, but can you blame me? I know you wanted to as well.*

Nathaniel Lewis: *I think I'm falling in love with you, Robin.*

The entire time I was reading, I held my breath. Was everything he was saying true? If it wasn't, then why would he send it in the first place? I could feel tears streaming down my face as I read the messages over and over. How could I be so stupid? I'd fallen in love with him too, and here I was on a plane to meet a guy I didn't even know. I felt sick.

"Mom, I need to go to the bathroom." I said abruptly, leaving my phone on the tray table and squeezing around her seat to the aisle. I stormed down the rows of seats toward the bathroom and practically slammed the door shut.

Suddenly, I felt myself losing my balance, and I knelt on the sticky bathroom floor and threw up into the toilet. I was so overwhelmed that my body was rejecting everything–like it was trying to expel the feelings by vomiting them out. What I did know was that it wasn't working.

A few minutes passed and I took a couple of deep breaths, flushing the toilet and wiping my eyes. Was I being an idiot? All I knew right now was that I wanted my mom.

I walked out of the tiny bathroom and past some concerned looking passengers who probably heard me hurl and made my way back to my seat. I sat back down and looked at Mom, who was nibbling on yet another croissant and suddenly I felt myself reach out and grab her for a hug as I began to sob.

Startled, she reached around me and hugged me back tightly. “Sweetie, what’s going on?” She asked, rubbing the back of my hair comfortingly.

“Boys are jerks.” I said, muffled into her sweatshirt through my tears. “Or maybe I’m the jerk, I don’t even know any more.”

She shushed me quietly and held me tight. “It’s okay.” She said.

Minutes past and I pulled away, taking a deep breath, and leaning back in my chair. I grabbed my phone and opened the messages from Nathaniel, showing them to Mom. She took the phone from me and began to read, her face not giving much away. I turned away from her and stared out the window at the clouds.

I felt her put the phone back on my tray table and then reach over and grab my hand, squeezing it tightly. “You know, we don’t have to see Mason on this trip...” She said, “we could just see the sights, then go home.”

I thought about this for a second but knew that wasn't an option.

"If I don't meet him, then I'll be stuck in this forever." I told her sincerely. "I want to know if what I've felt for the last three years with him has been real, or if-" I paused for a second, glancing down at the messages that were still lit up on my phone, "or if what I've been feeling with Nate is what I need to follow. It's felt more real these last few weeks with him than it ever did with Mason, but I owe him a chance..." I said, defeated.

Mom nodded and put her arm around me. "Right now, sweetie, all you have to think about is meeting Mason. Put Nate to the back of your head and remember that this is something you've been talking about for years. Don't let him spoil it for you."

I sighed. She was right. Without Nate in the picture, I would have been bouncing off the airplane walls with excitement. Mason was still the same guy I'd fallen for all those years ago, he was still the guy with the British accent that made me melt, and the dreams of theater we shared. He was worth trying for.

I shut my phone off, and Mom and I decided to have a movie marathon for the rest of the flight, watching whatever the plane had to offer.

I was so glad she was there.

Chapter 21

RobinM110: *Hello London!*

MPh2011: *Welcome to the land of tea and crumpets!*

"Okay, so..." Mom began as we both stared at the London Underground map in front of us. I had absolutely no idea what any of it meant and had a new respect for Mason for being able to understand any of it, let alone travel it. "By the looks of it, we need to go on this blue line here and then-" She paused, following the line with her finger, "then we get off and get on this yellow and pink line."

"No, no, because we need to get to the red one, so we stay on the blue one for longer, and we can go directly to the red one." I explained, trying to guide her along my route on the map.

"Yeah, but then we'll be going too far on the blue line and we'll have to come back on ourselves on the red one, so if we get on the pink and yellow one it should hypothetically save time... right?" Mom replied, looking completely confused.

"You know what would also save time?" I said, "getting a cab." I suggested.

"Good idea, fuck this." She said and I laughed.

"A dollar for the jar when we get home." I told her, putting on a strict voice and pointing disapprovingly at her.

"Oh please, I'm on vacation." She replied as we took the escalator back up to the Heathrow airport terminal and made our way outside into the British night time. It was coming up to midnight, but the airport was still very busy. We got in a line outside to queue for a cab and, after what felt like an eternity, we were on our way to the hotel.

"Where 'av you ladies come from then?" The driver asked in a thick cockney accent. I looked out the window at the city as Mom began to talk to him. I spotted a red phone box, and everyone was driving on the wrong side of the street. It was so cool being somewhere new, I couldn't wait to properly experience it, but right now, I was ready to get to the hotel and sleep in an actual bed.

As we drove, I looked down at my phone. Impulsively, I opened the messages from Nate. He said he was falling in love with me.

Nathaniel Lewis was falling in love with me. How was that even possible? We're both completely different people. Even if it were true, what was going to happen? We'd date for the summer maybe, then another girl would come along and grab his attention and before senior year even began I'd be back to being someone he didn't even acknowledge in the hallway, let alone someone he loved.

I hadn't responded, and I felt bad. He'd sent those messages into an abyss and if he were anything like me, he'd be checking his phone to see any hope of a response.

Lost in my thoughts, I hadn't even noticed us pull up outside the hotel. Bright lights lit up the entrance and a flickering sign above the door read 'The Fairwood Hotel'. It looked nice enough from the outside, but I wasn't here to judge hotels and as long as there was a bed and Wi-Fi, I was okay with it.

We manoeuvred our suitcases through the small entrance way and made our way up to the front desk where a woman, who couldn't have been much older than me, sat talking on her cell phone.

"Hold on a mo'" She said down the phone, placing it on the desk in front of her. "Welcome to The Fairwood 'otel, London's best kept secret, can I get your bookin' number and name please?" She said in the most monosyllabic tone I'd ever heard. Something tells me this wasn't her dream job.

"Oh, yes, it's Montgomery and the Booking is 758FH0LPY2" Mom read from a printed email she had at the ready. She was always very organised. I looked around and the hotel seemed more like a big house, and the hallway we were currently stood in was incredibly cramped to be a main entrance.

"Wonderful," the girl said, typing in the details to the computer. With the way she was talking you'd think us checking in was anything but 'wonderful'. She reached down below the desk and pulled out a key card for the room and handed it to Mom. "You're in room 17, 'ere's your key. Sometimes it doesn't work first time but just keep tryin'. Also, due to a health violation we're no longer permitted to serve breakfast in the mornin'." She said. Mom and I both looked at each other, concerned. "We don't do room service but if you need somethin' you can come 'ere, and someone should be able to 'elp." She explained.

"Great." Mom said, taking the key and looking at a sign on the wall that read 'Rooms 1–20' with an arrow. We followed it and made our way through the dim hallway, passing locked doors and a hotel room that was wide open for some reason. Mom slipped the key card in the door and it unlocked first try. "I'm so glad that worked, I didn't want to go and ask her for help." She said in a hushed voice. I laughed quietly.

The room itself wasn't bad. There were two double beds, a TV, a dressing table, and an en-suite bathroom which was small but manageable. On the table was a tray with an electric kettle, various types of tea and coffee and milk in tiny little containers. The towels were folded neatly on the end of the beds and there was a large window. I walked over and pulled the curtain aside. There was nothing spectacular to look at, just a parking lot, more buildings and a shop called 'Parkers' with no indication of what they sold.

"Well, this is cosy." Mom said, turning on the TV and switching through the channels. British accents hummed through the room from a news and weather channel that she ended up choosing.

I made myself comfortable on the bed closest to the window and plugged my phone into the outlet beside the bed with an adapter Mom bought in the airport when she realised that England has different outlets to us. "I don't know why there isn't just one universal outlet that everyone uses" she'd said to the cashier.

"Mom..." I said, leaning back on the bed and staring up at the ceiling, "Do you think I'm being stupid?" I asked before adding, "honestly..."

"What're you talking about?" She replied, perching down on the edge of the bed beside me and putting her hand on my knee. I sat up and looked at her.

"Nate literally just told me he thinks he's falling in love with me, and I'm sitting here ignoring him focussing on

Mason, and I've never even met Mason." I said, burying my face in my hands.

"Do you like Nate?" Mom asked. I sat silently then looked at her, she was looking me directly in the eye. I nodded in response. "Do you like Mason?" I paused then nodded again. "Then no, you're not being stupid." She said, "I think you've ended up in a situation you never expected, and I think you're struggling with understanding your feelings because for the last three years you've thought you'd be in love with Mason forever and now things aren't that easy anymore."

As she spoke, I nodded along. "Am I a bad person?" I asked without thinking. She smiled at me weakly.

"No honey, you're a teenage girl." She leaned over to me and kissed my forehead then stood up. "Now, I'm going to go call your Dad, let him know we're here safe. Maybe you should call Nate and talk to him, I know he'd probably appreciate a response. Or don't, that's okay too." She said. "We should be going to sleep soon though, so I'm not going to be long."

I decided it was better to not talk to Nate. If things went

well Mason tomorrow, then it would just hurt him more.

Holy shit, I'm meeting Mason tomorrow.

Chapter 22

RobinM110: *We're spending the day in London, let me know when you finish work!*

MPh2011: *Will do! I'm so excited!*

MPh2011: *I love you so much*

As we walked around London, Mom insisted on taking photographs of me in front of every tourist attraction. We took selfies together outside Buckingham Palace surrounded by crowds of people and, soon enough, I convinced Mom to let us walk through the West End and look at all the theatres. I took photos in front of huge *Hamilton* posters and *Dear Evan Hansen* marquees. It was beautiful. I was walking through heaven, and I could only imagine that this is what New York and Broadway would be like, but on a larger scale.

I couldn't believe that Mason came here every week and saw show after show. As I looked around, I realised that he'd walked these streets and maybe even stood in the same spots. My heart was beating so fast and I suddenly couldn't wait to meet him. Three years of my life had been leading to this moment and I wasn't going to let anyone ruin it.

"So, where do you want to go for lunch?" Mom asked as we took a seat on a bench near the theater that was currently housing *Les Misérables*.

"Well," I started, "I had one idea."

"And that would be?" Mom prompted.

"Mason works at a restaurant nearby... I'm so nervous, I kind of want to get this meeting over and done with, so we can just get to the next part of our relationship, you know?" I explained. "I know we agreed to meet when he finished work, but I just... think it could be fun to surprise him."

"If you think that's a good idea, then sure." Mom agreed, though she seemed reluctant. "Where does he work then?"

I looked around. "It's called The Townhouse Café" I said, grabbing my phone and opening my map to get directions. We followed the route and the closer we got the bigger the pit of nerves in my stomach became.

"Holy shit, I'm going to meet Mason." I mumbled. "I'm finally meeting my boyfriend, holy fucking shit." I said.

"Okay, I know I joked about being on vacation, but enough of the language, Robin." Mom said, looking around the streets. "Hey, there it is." She said, pointing at a sandwich board that stood outside a small café. I definitely wouldn't have called it a restaurant but, I guessed that might have been a British thing.

I looked at it in the distance and found myself unable to move suddenly. Was I ready for this? Could I walk in there, meet the guy I believed to be the love of my life, and tell him I kissed another guy just last week? I felt sick with nerves, excitement, dread, guilt, every emotion I think I'd ever felt. I noticed myself shaking and Mom put her hands on my shoulders.

"You've got this." She said, smiling.

I took a deep breath. "I've got this."

We made our way to the café and slowly we walked in. It was quaint, nothing special, and I couldn't really picture West End stars coming here after a long show day like Mason claimed but maybe it was quite a popular place. Although, it was a Saturday at lunchtime, and it was practically empty.

We walked up to the counter displaying cakes, pastries, and sandwiches where a cashier stood looking bored. "Um... hey..." I said, awkwardly.

"Can I get you anything?" The boy asked, looking across at me.

"I was just wondering if Mason was here?" I asked and he looked confused.

"Sorry?"

"Mason? Is Mason here?" I repeated.

The boy looked at me, almost lost. "Uh, there's no one called Mason who works here."

"What?" Mom said, concerned.

"It's just me, Alissa, Tony and Peppa at the moment." He said and I felt my heart drop. What was happening? "So, can I get you anything?" He repeated. I hesitated then walked away and grabbed a seat at a nearby table, grabbing my phone and pulling up my conversation with Mason.

RobinM110: *Are you at work? I wanted to surprise you but there's no sign of you.*

Mom walked over with a tray with a glass of orange juice and a pot of English tea, placing them both down on the table. I grabbed the orange juice and took a sip, staring at my phone. I tapped my fingers anxiously against the table and I could feel Mom staring at me. I continued to refresh my messages with Mason. Even when he was at work normally, he'd be able to respond, this was getting weird.

Suddenly, as I saw a pop up saying he'd read the message, we heard a crash in the kitchen. We bolted our heads round and tried to get any sense of what had happened but couldn't see anything.

That's when a guy came walking out of the back room, around the counter and toward us, keeping his eyes locked on me the entire time. I felt almost exposed, like I'd done something wrong.

"Robin..." He said and I looked at him, eyebrow raised and worry now taking over every other feeling. Mom looked at me, then at the man who stood in front of us. I stood up, walking toward him cautiously.

He had long messy blonde hair; dark, piercing eyes and a tattoo on his lower arm of what looked like a Pokémon, but I wasn't sure. He was tall, with glasses and wearing a t-shirt that looked like it said '*The Book of Mormon*' but it was obscured by his apron.

"I can't believe it's you." He said, staring at me intensely.

I'd pictured this moment a thousand times over the last three years. I thought about running toward him and hugging him. I wondered what our first kiss would be like, whether he would see me and instantly kiss me, or if we'd go on a date – maybe a candlelit dinner after a visit to the theater – and he'd walk me home or to my hotel and kiss me softly at the end of the night.

I expected my instincts to take over the moment I saw him, like they did with Florence, and we'd hold each other tight, but this wasn't what I expected. My throat felt tight, my heart was pounding, and my instincts were telling me to run.

Because it was Mason... but... this wasn't Mason.

I hesitated. "You're... Mason?" I asked, feeling the blood rush to my cheeks. I wanted to cry.

I saw him hesitate. "Well, actually, it's Tony." He admitted. I felt sick.

"Is this some kind of sick joke?" Mom said, and I don't think I'd ever heard her so angry. She stood up beside me and looked at Mas- Tony.

"Mom..." I said. "It's... it's okay." I told her as I took a step closer to the man who stood in front of me. I looked deep into his eyes. The voice was the same one I'd heard for three years, but his looks, his whole face, everything was different. "What's going on?" I asked after what felt like a lifetime of silence.

"Can we sit and talk? Please?" He pleaded. I looked back at Mom and I could see she was furious with the situation. I walked over to another empty table and Tony followed me. I sat down, and he took a seat opposite me.

"I... okay, well, first I want to say sorry." He started, but I couldn't look at him. He reached out, trying to take my hand, but I pulled away and he retreated. "I never meant for any of this to go this far and I thought if we finally got to meet you might see that I'm a good guy and not just a liar."

I continued to stare at the table, refusing to look in his eyes.

"I always wanted to tell you the truth but I just-"

"What is the truth?" I interrupted, looking up at the stranger in front of me angrily. I was done with games. No more lies, no more hiding my feelings.

"Well, my name's Tony-"

I slammed my hands on the table, frustrated. "I know that. What else?" I demanded.

He looked at me, his eyes sad, but I just didn't care. "I'm not actually eighteen. I'm 24. I live with my parents; I don't have my own flat. I dropped out of university and I ended up spending loads of time online, that's when we started talking..." He admitted. I wanted to throw up.

"So, when we started talking, you were a 21-year-old college dropout and you started a relationship with a naive 14-year-old? I was a child." I said, frankly. "And these last few weeks of telling me I just *had* to come and study here so we could be together? What was all that? Some ploy to get me here without my mom so you could what? Take advantage of me? Prey on your little victim? You're a fucking predator." I felt my voice raising as I continued to talk.

"No! Of course not!" He said. "It's not like I'm some 50-year-old pervert. I had this whole plan, okay? We were going to go for dinner and I was going to bring you a rose and take you to a show and make you see I'm the same person you've been talking to this whole time but I just... look different." He explained but the pit in my stomach seemed to be getting bigger and bigger. "I found someone who I had things in common with. I felt something and I know you did too." At this point, I noticed the rest of the staff were watching on from behind the counter.

"I felt something when I thought I was talking to another kid my age!" I shouted. "Fuck this, I'm leaving." I said, standing up from my chair abruptly and storming out of the café.

I wanted to run and hide but everywhere I looked was alien to me. The buildings were no longer quaint to me, they were walls to a prison I couldn't leave. The people on the streets weren't just people, they were strangers. This whole place was a mystery. I felt someone behind me, and Mom grabbed me in a tight hug.

"Sweetie, I am so proud of you. I am so, so, so proud of you." She said, holding me in a tight embrace on the streets of an unknown city. Before I could stop myself, I burst into tears, sobbing into her chest.

"I'm so stupid." I mumbled through the tears against her shirt. "I'm so fucking stupid." I sobbed, pulling away from her hug and beginning to walk away from the café.

Suddenly, I heard footsteps trailing after us and I turned around. Tony was there trying to catch up. Mom stepped in front of me.

"I want you to leave my daughter alone, do you hear me?" She said to him as he caught his breath.

"Mrs. Montgomery, please, let me talk to Robin, please." He pleaded. I couldn't even bring myself to look at him. "You've talked to me before; you know I'm a good guy." He added.

"I am seconds away from slapping you, boy, so you better walk away and fast." Mom told him. There was a pause and when I looked up, the stranger I thought I knew was walking away.

Chapter 23

MPh2011: *Please talk to me.*

MPh2011: *I just need some time to explain.*

MPh2011: *So, it's over, just like that?*

MPh2011: *I'm not letting it end this way.*

I stood in the cramped shower of our tiny hotel bathroom and let the tears stream down my face. How could I have let this happen? I'd poured out my hopes and dreams to that man. He'd heard me cry and complain about high school and life and here he was lying his ass off the entire time. Not only that, but I let him get in my head so much that I might have ruined any chance I had of even being friends with Nate now. I just wanted to go home.

When my fingers started to look wrinkly, I climbed out of the shower, wrapping myself in a warm hotel towel. I just couldn't believe he was lying this entire time. Was I...

a victim? I shuddered and shook the thought from my head, getting dressed into my pyjamas. I wanted to go to sleep, get through the next day and fly home. I wanted to cuddle Munchkin and watch a movie with Dad. I wanted to be anywhere but here.

"Robin..." Mom called through the bathroom door, knocking softly as she did.

"I'll be out in a minute." I said, rubbing my hair with a towel. I wiped my blood-shot eyes and sighed. Fuck this day.

As I walked out of the bathroom, I noticed Mom perched on the edge of her bed looking surprisingly smiley. "What did you do?" I asked, half-expecting her to say she'd gone out while I was showering and punched Mason- or Tony, in the face.

"I know that today has been... well, not what you'd hoped, so I've got something to cheer you up." She said, "Drumroll please..." She snickered and I immediately thought of Nate. I thought of that day we'd spent at The Kingfisher. The day he'd watched me dance. I would give anything to go back to that. I sighed, tapping a slow drumroll on my legs.

From behind her back, she revealed some folded pieces of paper. “Please tell me those are plane tickets, and we’re going home right now?” I asked optimistically.

“Nope,” she said, unfolding the paper. “These are tickets to see *42nd Street* the musical tonight on the West End.” She grinned.

“You’re shitting me?” I blurted out. “Seriously?”

“Language. And no, I’m not ‘shitting you’. I bought them so you could go with Mason on a date, but obviously that’s not going to happen, and I know how much you love the dancing in this show, so I figured it could be a nice mother and daughter evening on the town.” She explained.

I ran over to her and hugged her tight. “You’re amazing.” I could feel my eyes welling up again.

“I know.” She agreed. “Now get ready, we’re going to try the Tube again. I think I’ve got the route nailed.”

“Mom, I love you, but please can we just get a cab? I don’t want to be late.” I asked and she rolled her eyes.

"Nope, we're doing this." She laughed, giving me another quick hug.

Maybe today wouldn't be so bad after all...

As we queued outside the theater, I couldn't stop myself from humming some of the songs from the show quietly to myself. I thought about what it would have been like to be here with Mason- *my* Mason, not fake Mason, then realised that was never going to be possible. I sighed.

I'd pictured seeing a West End show for years. Mason and I had talked about it endlessly. We'd sit in the front row, staring at the actors as we got pulled into their world and admiring the costumes, the story, the talent. I'd dreamed of those moments. Now I was never going to have them with him.

We had our bags checked as we entered the theater and immediately my eyes were drawn to the merchandise stand and I dragged Mom behind me. "Can I get something?" I asked, pleadingly. "I'll pay." I added quickly, looking at the t-shirts and sweatshirts, the mugs, and the key chains.

Mom simply nodded, looking at me with a weak smile. She looked sympathetic... almost like she was pitying me.

I ended up buying a black t-shirt with the show logo on the front, a large hooded sweatshirt, and a programme for the show. As we made our way up the stairs to our seats, I flipped through it, admiring the photographs and actor's bios. One day I hoped to be in one of these for a professional production.

"You don't mind that we're in the nosebleed section, right?"

"Mom, we could be standing in the merch line through the entire show and I wouldn't mind." I told her sincerely.

We took our seats and I looked down at the stage. The velvet red curtain fell perfectly across the stage and I could feel myself grinning wide.

"This is so cool."

Mom took the program from me and started flicking through it. I grabbed the t-shirt I bought out of mom's bag and pulled it over my head, the smile still wide on my face.

"I'm so excited."

The lights began to dim, and the overture started to play, then I found myself getting lost in a world of tap dancing and music for the next 2 and a half hours. I didn't exist outside this room. This was where I belonged.

Too soon the show ended, and the cast began to bow. I stood up and clapped my hands vigorously, cheering along with the rest of the crowd. The show was incredible, it epitomised everything I loved about theater, and if I could dance in a production like this one day, I'd be so happy. I watched as the curtain closed and I had to go back to my reality. A reality of no sequins and costumes, no bright pink tap shoes, or big solos–just a reality of catfishes and confusing quarterbacks.

People began squeezing past me in the aisle to leave but I couldn't bring myself to follow. I didn't want to go back to my life. The last 2 hours were the best and least stressed I'd had in weeks.

"Come on, sweetie, we should go." Mom said, patting me on the back and leading me out of the aisle of seats to the exit.

We made our way out of the theater into the cold London air. I shivered as I watched the theatregoers walk down the street. Mom followed them and took my hand. Since the meeting with Tony earlier she seemed far more protective, she took my hand the entire time wc were on the London Underground on the way to the theater, and she kept her arm around me practically the whole way through the show. It was like she was treating me like a child.

Mom seemed to know the route through the Underground expertly this time and it made me wonder if she'd spent most of the show figuring out the way back–it wouldn't surprise me if she had.

"Thank you so much by the way." I said, resting my head on Mom's shoulder looking up at the Underground maps that were plastered across the train carriage.

"That's okay. This trip isn't a total bust." She said as a slightly-real-slightly-robotic voice announced we were approaching our stop. "We've had a good time, regardless of... well, you know."

"Mom," I started, "can you do something for me?" I asked. "I know it's like, a big thing, but can you just not tell Dad about Mason? Can you just tell him that it didn't feel right or that I realised I'm falling in love with Nate instead or something?" I asked. "He won't ever trust me to go on the internet again or trust me to leave for college or anything. I don't want a stupid mistake I made talking to some guy online when I was fourteen make him not trust me, you know?" We walked out of the station and onto the street as she smiled to herself. "What?" I asked.

"I'm not going to not tell your Dad what happened, but I'll make sure he doesn't do anything you said. Moving on though," she said, turning in the direction of the hotel, "do you realize what you just said?"

I glanced at her, confused, and shook my head. "Um... I don't know?"

"I think you just admitted that you've fallen for Nate." She said and I stopped walking, shocked at my own admission and the completely casual way I said it. Maybe everything that happened with 'Mason', or Tony, or whoever, wasn’t completely awful. It made me realize the truth about my situation.

I did love Nate.

Chapter 24

MPh2011: *Robin please*

RobinM110: *Leave me alone.*

We spent the next day visiting tourist attractions across the city. I tried to enjoy it as much as I could now that I didn't have the anticipation of meeting 'Mason' to worry about, but something still lingered. I didn't like knowing I was still in the same city as him. My heart hurt when I thought about it. I felt like I'd been taken advantage of. I mean, it's not like anything ever happened and I'm thankful that Mom was there when we met but I feel like I'd been robbed of part of my youth.

Mom decided we should take a trip on the London Eye and as we stood there in this glass ball looking out over the city, I felt the tears welling up in my eyes. I looked out at the streets and the strange array of buildings, some old, some still being built. A place that held so much history yet was still changing, and now a huge part of my history was going to live here forever. I met the first person I ever loved in those streets, and it came crashing down around me. How could I have let that happen? I look back at all the stupid mistakes I made and cringe at the thoughts. Every time we video chatted it was always so dark on his webcam that I could barely see his face but I didn't even mind–he always told me it was late, and he was about to head to sleep and I'd just blindly believed in him. I learned my lesson at least, don't blindly believe anyone.

I wiped the tears from my eyes and held my phone up to take a photo of the view. London was a beautiful place, and under different circumstances I think I would have absolutely adored it. I could have even seen myself living here, but the idea that this Tony person was here, and I could run into him at any moment frightened me. I was genuinely scared.

Our plane was leaving later tonight, at 2am, so we decided to grab an early dinner from a pub near to the hotel before checking out and making our way to the airport ("on the tube as they say!" Mom had said). Mom decided to have the 'bangers and mash' while I had the 'fish and chips' ... when in Rome and all. It was nice, but I was ready to get back to Colorado. England had been a bit of a culture shock, amongst other shocks.

As I packed and Mom took a "much needed" bath, I checked my phone. Since meeting Tony, he'd barely stopped messaging me from his 'Mason' account and in the last minute he'd barely stopped.

MPh2011: *Robin this is ridiculous.*

MPh2011: *Can't we just call and talk about this?*

MPh2011: *You're going to talk to me.*

MPh2011: *I'm outside the hotel. I'll be waiting.*

Panicked, I messaged back:

RobinM110: *Leave before I call the cops because I will.*

Honestly, it was an empty threat. I had no intention of calling the police or adding more drama to this situation, especially since I would be getting on a plane in a few hours and I wouldn't have to ever see him again. I wondered how long he would stay there for. If he came to the room, Mom would go ballistic and if we left the hotel and he was waiting outside then she wouldn't hesitate to call the cops and then who knows how long we'd be stuck in London dealing with whatever happened.

Quietly, I listened at the bathroom door. Mom was loudly watching Netflix on her phone as she bathed, so I knew I had some time on my own. I took a breath, pulled on my old worn-out sneakers, and grabbed the room key. Why the hell was I doing this?

I made my way through the small hotel to the front entrance where, through the door, I could see Tony perched on the front step. My heart sank.

"You need to leave." I said as I walked outside behind him. His head shot around quickly, and I looked at the stranger staring back at me. He was similar to the photos he'd sent me, but just different enough for me to look at every part of him and remember what a liar he turned out to be.

"Robin" He said, standing up and taking a step toward me.

"Stay over there." I instructed, and he retreated. "What do you want from me?" I asked as I held my phone tight in my jacket pocket, it was the one I'd bought tonight at the show. "You got what you wanted. You made me out to look like a fucking fool, you manipulated me into coming here, tried to get me to move in with you when you knew that you had been lying this whole time and now what? Do you want me to say it's okay? That I forgive you?" I ranted. "It doesn't work like that."

"I know." He said. I looked past the big hipster glasses on his nose and stared into his eyes. His eyes were blood shot and he looked like he'd been crying. "I just- I couldn't let you leave tomorrow without properly talking to you." He pleaded. "Please."

I stared at him, looking at him up and down. He gripped his phone in his hand and I noticed he still had the page with our messages open on his screen. I looked at the tattoo on his arm then noticed that his knuckles looked slightly bruised.

"What did you do?" I asked, casually, crossing my arms across my chest and staring at his hand.

"Oh... I punched the wall of the café after you left. I was angry." He explained. I felt myself back away instinctively. Seeing his bruised hand made me instantly more uncomfortable–did he have anger issues he hadn't told me about? He must have noticed too because he quickly said, "I'm not going to hurt you or anything." as I moved.

We both stared at each other for a moment, then he took a seat on the front step. Cautiously, I walked toward him and followed suit, sitting down a couple of feet away. "Why did you do it?" I asked.

"Punch the wall?"

"No. Why did you talk to me and lead me on all this time?" I questioned. He stared down at his lap, squeezing his hands together so tight they looked like they were turning white.

He sighed. "It got out of hand."

I rolled my eyes. "Do you know how many Catfish episodes I've seen where they say that?" I shot back.

"It's true." He argued. "I made the account because I wanted to meet people who liked the same things I did. The same reason anyone goes on Geeks Haven."

"Not everyone lies about their name and age and who they really are though." I told him.

"I never lied about who I am. I mean, sure, the technical things like my name and stuff but I never lied about anything we talked about. That was always me." He said and I tore my eyes away from him. I stared out at the street which was quiet aside from a few cars driving past every few minutes.

"My name is Tony McPhilips, that's where the username came from, my last name." He explained. "And we talked for ages before we said how old we were and-"

"How old *I* was." I corrected.

"You told me you were fourteen, I didn't want to seem like a creep, so I lied and said I was fifteen. I didn't see any harm at the time, but then I got to know you and things changed."

I gritted my teeth and clenched my fists. "I was a child." I mumbled, feeling my tears welling up again. I was so fed up of crying.

"Everything I ever said to you was real, Robin, you have to believe that." He said. As I wasn't looking at him, all I could hear was his voice. It was the same voice I'd fallen for all those years ago with the accent I'd melted at just a couple of months ago. It was the voice of a liar.

"What about when you said you were going to fly out at the weekend to meet me? Then changed your mind and basically forced me out here? What was your plan then?" I probed. "Turn up at my door and tell me the truth and expect me to invite you in with open arms?"

He stayed silent for a second. "I wasn't sure. It was impulsive and then when I thought it through, I realised that was a stupid idea. That's when I started asking you to come here."

"Asking me? More like demanding." I shot back.

I hadn't even notice him edge closer to me and, when I turned around to look at him, I felt his mouth crash against mine. I was taken aback and for a second, I wasn't sure what was going on and felt myself kiss back instinctively.

When I realised what was happening, that this stranger was kissing me, I pulled away. We stared at each other and before I could stop myself, I slapped him hard across the face. My palm was instantly stinging from the impact.

I stood up and backed away, toward the door to the hotel. "Robin, I'm sorry, I-"

"Get away from me." I yelled a little louder than I'd intended.

"I couldn't let you go without a kiss."

I let out a breath and shook my head in disbelief. "You're a fucking predator. You're a disgusting fucking liar and I want you out of my life."

At this, I stormed back into the hotel and practically sprinted back to the room. I turned back to check that he wasn't following me and tried the key card three times before it decided to finally unlock. When I closed the door, I heard Mom still in the bathroom, and I fell to my knees, finally letting out the sobs I had been holding back.

I reached into my pocket, grabbed my phone, and deleted my Geeks Haven account without a moment's hesitation. That's when, through my tears, I noticed a new message from Nate.

Nathaniel Lewis: *I'm sorry I put all that on you the other day. It wasn't fair.*

I let out another sob then pressed the call button before I even noticed what I was doing. It rang a few times, and for a second, I thought about hanging up but then I heard his voice.

“Hey...” He said hesitantly and I felt my whole body relax more than it had all weekend. I tried to compose myself, sniffing and wiping away my tears, as if he could see me. I had been sobbing so badly I could barely catch my breath.

“Robin, what’s going on?” He asked, sounding concerned. He could clearly tell I wasn’t myself.

“I love you.” I blurted out, shocking myself. There was silence on the end of the line. “I love you, I love you, I love you.” I repeated and I couldn’t stop myself. Any filter I had was gone. There was still no response, for a second, I thought he could have been disconnected, but I heard him breathe. “Everything between us was more real than I ever expected or planned for it to be. I don’t know how it happened, but I’m so glad it did, and I’m so damn sorry that I ever pushed you away for someone else because you are more than enough for me. You’re one of the best people I've ever met and you get me and when you kissed me I just never wanted it to end and everything I ever thought love was is nothing compared to the way I feel about you." I rambled between sobs. I could still feel Tony's lips against mine and it made me feel sick. I wiped my mouth on my arm. I wish I could take back that whole relationship.

"Slow down, little lady." He said and I could practically hear him smirking down the phone. As I steadied my breathing and wiped away the tears, we sat in silence on the phone.

"I love you too, dummy." He said after what felt like an eternity. I smiled, sniffing a little. There was another pause, "but what happened with your British boy?" I felt my stomach turn at the mention of him. He could still be outside for all I knew.

"He..." I started with a sigh. I thought better of explaining the whole thing over the phone. "I don't want to talk about that right now, is that okay?" I asked. "I'll tell you all about it when I get home."

"Okay. When are you back?" He asked.

"Our plane leaves in..." I paused, checking the time. "Six hours," I said. "Then it's about 12 hours on the plane so that's going to be around tomorrow morning for you, I think... I'm not sure, I'm pretty exhausted." I admitted. "It's been the longest weekend ever."

"What have you been up to then?" He asked, and we ended up talking for the next couple of hours while I finished packing my bags.

Mom had said hi down the phone, told him to give her love to his parents and then left us to it as she watched some British game show. I told him how we saw all the sights, that we went on the London Eye and I got to see Buckingham Palace and I raved for probably too long about seeing 42nd Street.

"Robin's going to have to go now!" Mom said, leaning over my shoulder and talking down the phone herself. "We have to get the Tube to the airport, because *I know* how to use the Tube and our plane leaves in a couple of hours." She said and I heard Nate laugh down the phone and I rolled my eyes at her.

"Subtle brag there, Mom." I commented, and she simply shrugged as she switched off the TV and made sure one last time that we'd packed everything. "Okay well... I'll see you in like... 16 hours." I said. We both hesitated, leaving a silence hanging in the air.

"Okay..." He said. His voice was soft and quiet. "I love you." I heard him say and my heart started beating so fast I thought it might explode. I still couldn't believe Nathaniel Lewis was saying that to me.

I looked over at Mom who was still checking all the outlets and making sure she hadn't left behind any hotel toiletries, then just as quietly I replied, "I love you too." with a smile. Mom shot her head round to me with a grin wider than I'd seen in years and I shrugged guiltily. This was going to be an interesting flight home.

Chapter 25

*The account '**RobinM110**' no longer exists.*
Click here to sign up.

All the way to the airport, Mom had been asking questions about Nate. She was asking how it happened, what our first kiss was like, basically everything I didn't want to talk to Mom about. Eventually, she'd let the topic go and started asking me about Tony. I still didn't know whether to tell her what had happened earlier that evening. When we sat in the airport, waiting for our plane to start boarding, I finally brought the subject up.

"He came to the hotel." I stated simply. Mom looked at me, confused. "Mason- I mean, Tony. He came to the hotel." I explained further. Mom's face seemed to drop.

"And you didn't tell me, why?" She asked, accusingly. I could tell she was mad.

"You were watching some romcom in the bath." I said, as if that was a reasonable excuse. "It's fine, I mean, I'm fine." I reassured her. "I slapped him."

"You *what?*" She replied, shocked. "Wait, let me get this straight, you secretly saw this man behind my back and then assaulted him?"

Awkwardly, I nodded. "Only after he kissed me though." Immediately, I regretted saying that. Before she had a chance to lose her mind, I continued, "he said he wanted to talk to me. I felt like I owed him that much since we'd been talking for so long."

"Robin, you don't owe him anything. That man took advantage of you for years, then stalked you to our hotel then-" She paused, almost looking sad. She grabbed me and pulled me in for a tight hug and I hugged her back. "I'm glad you slapped him because if saw him again I would have done a lot worse."

I nodded, feeling her warmth against me, and sighed. "I know I don't owe him anything. Don't worry, I gave him a piece of my mind." I said. "I'm stronger than you think, Mom."

“I know you are,” she started, “but Robin...” She paused and her tone dropped. “You’ve been a victim of something I couldn’t imagine and now he... kissing you... that’s sexual assault. He was an adult talking to a child and now this... I think we need to tell the police.”

“Mom, please, I don’t want to do that.” I begged. “I don’t want anything to do with him ever again. I just want to go home and move on with my life.” I pleaded.

I thought about what she said. I never considered a kiss to be assault, and I’d pictured kissing Mason many times, but this wasn’t Mason and it wasn’t something I’d wanted to happen.

“I’m your Mom, I’m supposed to be able to protect you, but I let this man into your life, and I let it happen and now this... I’m just so disappointed in myself.” She said as an announcement said we could now board our flight.

“You never could have known, Mom.” I reassured her. “Please don’t blame yourself.”

In silence, we embraced again then made our way onto the flight.

All I wanted to do was go to sleep.

I woke up on the flight and looked around, taking in my surroundings and yawning. I noticed Mom was asleep while a movie I didn't recognise played through her earphones then I pulled out my phone and connected to the Wi-Fi.

It buzzed a few times and I checked my notifications. A few messages lit up the screen.

Florence Hammersmith: *Why can't I find you on Geeks Haven? What's going on? You haven't talked to me all weekend, did the meeting with Mason go okay? I'm worried. Please message me.*

Nathaniel Lewis: *Thinking about you*

Mason Carlisle: *Please don't shut me out.*

Daniella Sweet: *How come you didn't tell me you were going to London!!! Saw your insta pics, so cool!!!*

Dad: *Miss you sweetie. Will be picking you up from the airport at 7am*

Firstly, I opened the conversation with 'Mason', removed him as a friend and blocked him on every social media I could find, then blocked his phone number. I was done with him.

Next, I finally messaged Florence:

Robin Montgomery: *I'm so sorry I haven't been in contact, been a really hectic few days. Had to delete my Geeks Haven account, Mason was a fake. His real name is Tony, he's 24 not 18, and he's a creep. He followed me to my hotel then tried to kiss me. I gave him a hard slap to the face, called him a predator and blocked him on all social media and deleted my Geeks Haven just to be sure. It was such a blur and in a panic, it didn't really occur to me to message you, I just wanted him gone, you know? I'm okay though. On the flight home now, ready to get back to normality.*

Robin Montgomery: *Oh, also, Nate told me he loved me.*

Robin Montgomery: *And I said it back.*

Robin Montgomery: *A lot to digest.*

I checked the time in New York and realised it would have been past 1am, so I didn't expect a response right away. I ignored Daniella's message, I figured I'd speak to her when I got home anyway, then messaged Dad telling him I couldn't wait to see him too and then Nate.

Robin Montgomery: *I'm thinking of you too.*

I paused before typing another message:

Robin Montgomery: *Thinking of your eyes and your smile and our kiss. God, I want to kiss you again.*

I let out a contented sigh and pressed send. Maybe it was my tired mind giving me the confidence to send that, either way I couldn't stop smiling at my phone. Soon enough, I had a response.

Nathaniel Lewis: *you can't send me messages like that while I'm in bed, it makes the mind wander to some dangerous places.*

I blushed.

Robin Montgomery: *You think I'm dangerous? ;)*

Nathaniel Lewis: *I'm starting to...*

Robin Montgomery: *Is dangerous good?*

Nathaniel Lewis: *it could be...*

Nathaniel Lewis: *but not when you're at 20,000 feet and I'm in bed.*

Robin Montgomery: *Okay, I'll let you sleep. I'm going to try and sleep more too, even though that's going to be hard when all I'm thinking about is being close to you.*

Nathaniel Lewis: *Soon, little lady.*

I smirked down at my phone and before I knew it, I'd fallen asleep again.

The hours ticked by far too slow for my liking. I wanted to be back on the ground and come out of this weekend on the other side because while I was in the air, my brain just kept going back to 'Mason'. I glanced at the clock on the screen in front of me, we had three hours to go. I could easily kill some time with a movie, or even listen to a long musical soundtrack, but I just couldn't get myself to focus on any one thing.

One moment I felt like I was on cloud nine, looking down at my messages to Nate and scrolling through his Instagram staring at his beautiful face; or I'd be thinking about the kiss we shared at the reservoir and my mind would flash to Tony and I felt like throwing up again. But no, I was not going to vomit in two airplane bathrooms in less than a week. I had some pride.

My mom's words repeated in my head like a siren. *"He took advantage of you"* and *"that's sexual assault"* on a loop going round and round non-stop. This was someone I trusted wholeheartedly and now all that had been thrown away in an instant. That moment where he walked out in the café and said my name was like a stab to the stomach, and I was feeling it over and over.

Trying to shake the thoughts away, I scrolled through Nate's Facebook profile. I looked at photos of him from football games, pep rallies, parties. I looked at the photos of us from the party and I stared at the blurry moment I danced with him. Before I knew it, I was looking through photos of him and Georgina and the rest of his friends.

All these people were so different to me. I was merely another face in a crowd of hundreds that they ignored. They cheered at the pep rallies and played the football games with him while I watched from the sidelines, sang in school assemblies and stood at the back of the glee club.

Suddenly, it felt like the only person in my life that fully understood me was Florence, and she was so far away from me. How could I face Nate knowing that, when we get back to reality, he'll just brush me off again like he did before?

I switched my phone off and buried my head in my hands, leaning against the tray table.

"Honey, what's up?" Mom asked, gently rubbing my back. "I thought you were excited to be going back home?"

I hesitated. "I am... I just, don't know what I'm doing." I admitted.

"What do you mean?" She prompted.

I let out a large sigh, running my fingers back through my hair and holding my hands against the back of my neck. I watched the little animation of a cartoon plane on the screen in front of me as it edged ever so slightly closer to Denver.

"Nate's just going to blow me off, it's inevitable."

Mom shook her head. "What are you talking about? You just told each other you love one another." She said. "He's not going to blow you off."

"Yes, he is. He has before." I admitted. "And we're such different people, like, he's the quarterback for God's sake and I'm what? Some nobody?" I rambled.

"That's just your mind running rampant." Mom said calmly.

"Is it?" I asked. "Mason-" I let out a groan before correcting myself. "*Tony* was a liar, who's to say Nate's not lying too? What if this is some messed up prank and I've just fallen for it?"

"Come here..." She said, putting her arm around me and pulling me into her. I rested on her and relaxed. "We both know Nate isn't that type of person."

I mumbled, "I didn't think Mason was that type of person either."

I felt her nod against me. "I know, and what happened with him was really bad, but you can't let that ruin everyone else for you." She said. I knew she was right.

I did love Nate, and if he said he loved me too then I was going to believe him. He wasn't the type to lie like that... at least, I hoped he wasn't.

I spotted Dad in a small crowd of people holding signs and noticed he was holding one that said 'My two favorite girls' and I smiled. We walked over, suitcases dragging behind us, and he gave us both a massive hug. “Oh, I’ve missed you guys” He said, squeezing us hard and causing mom’s suitcase handle to jab me in the stomach.

“You’ve spent longer in the office before than we did in London.” I joked and he grinned widely.

“True,” He said, taking my suitcase from me and wheeling it behind him instead, “but when you’re in a different country it’s just so much worse.” He said, leaning over and kissing Mom on the cheek. I smiled. It was so nice to be back.

We packed our bags in the trunk of the car and I climbed in the back. “Now, I can’t believe I’ve been with you for more than 30 seconds and you haven’t already told me how amazing it all was.” He prompted.

Mom looked back at me from the passenger’s seat and I shrugged, not knowing whether to tell him the truth. I knew she hated keeping secrets from him, and it would come out eventually, but I stayed silent.

“Well, London is absolutely gorgeous.” Mom began as Dad set off driving. “We went on the London Eye, the theater was beautiful, they even have those red phone boxes that you see in movies but none of them seem to actually work." She said. "Oh, and, the most important thing! I learnt how to use the Tube!" She exclaimed and we all laughed. "I'm an expert. I know that the Piccadilly line is the red one and the-"

"Piccadilly was blue, Mom." I interrupted. "The red one was Central."

"Well, regardless, I got us to and from where we needed to be and absolutely nailed it." She boasted.

There was a silence for a few moments. "And... Mason?" Dad asked. Mom stayed silent and I glanced at Dad in the rear-view mirror.

"He um..." I started. "He wasn't exactly what I was expecting." I said. It wasn't a lie. "Plus, I think my mind was elsewhere, but I'm tired so can I nap on the ride home and you guys just chat?" I asked. I had no intention of napping, but sometimes it was an easy way to get out of a conversation.

"Oh... okay." Dad said. I watched as Mom put her hand on my dad's thigh and squeezed it. They always made love look so easy.

I grabbed my earphones from my sweatshirt pocket and plugged them into my phone, then scrolled through my music to find the 42nd Street soundtrack. As I listened to the music play, I thought of the dancers and the costumes and the wonder of the theater. Listening to the music wouldn't ever compare to seeing it live, but it was close enough.

Just then, I realised I never took my phone off of airplane mode and as I did, I got a burst of messages through from Florence.

Florence Hammersmith: *That was a lot to process, but I'm going to say this: FUCK MASON. FUCK TONY. FUCK WHOEVER. HE'S AN ASS AND DOESN'T DESERVE YOUR AMAZINGNESS IN HIS LIFE.*

Florence Hammersmith: *Okay, now that's out of my system... I'm sorry that happened Boo. You really are amazing, and you deserve the world.*

Florence Hammersmith: *And I know I only spoke to him for a short time, but Nate seems like he wants to try and give you the world.*

Florence Hammersmith: *Now if you'll excuse me, I'm going to go and message this Tony guy, give him a piece of my mind, then report him to the Geeks Haven admins.*
Love you Boo

At least I knew one thing for certain, Florence would always have my back and I think that's settled it for me: New York was where I needed to be. It was time to re-think my college list.

All the way home I found myself searching for musical theater and dance programs through New York and was so engrossed in reading about courses that I'd barely noticed us arrive in Fort Collins. I'd even found myself looking at football scholarships for New York universities... you know... just in case.

We made our way through town and my heart was beating so fast in the anticipation to see Nate. I was beyond ready for this moment. I felt my leg shaking with adrenaline and quickly checked the time–it wasn't even 9am, so I wasn't sure he'd even be awake yet.

We arrived, Dad parked the car in our driveway, and I bolted out, practically sprinting next door. As I made my way across Nate's lawn, the front door opened and there he was, like he had been waiting.

I stopped just shy of the front steps, taking him in. Nate was still wearing his pyjama pants and wore a loose striped t-shirt. His hair was a mess, he looked tired and yet, he looked amazing. "Hi..." I said, unable to stop myself from grinning ear to ear.

"Little lady..." He smiled back. I could see he was eyeing me up and down like he always did, and I didn't even care that I was wearing the same leggings and sweatshirt I had been wearing in London. I didn't care that my hair was in the messiest ponytail ever or that my makeup had faded after 12 hours on a plane.

I couldn't wait any longer. I climbed the steps and fell into his embrace. I wrapped my arms around his neck, and he held me by the waist with one arm and held the back of my head with his other hand, trailing his fingers in my messy blonde hair. "I love you." He mumbled into my ear and I pulled away, looking him in the eyes.

Then it happened. I kissed him. I kissed him so hard I thought we were going to lose our balance. I felt him wrap his arms around my waist and pick me up off the floor. This was what I'd wanted all summer. I never wanted Mason; I never knew him. Nate was everything I ever wanted, and I hadn't even realised. As we kissed, I ran my hands through his hair and held him so tight I never wanted to let go.

When we finally broke away from one another for air, I looked him in the eyes and said, "I love you too."

Chapter 26

*The account **'MPh2011'** has been suspended.*

"So, do you want to talk about what happened in London?" Nate asked as we took a seat on the edge of his bed. It was weird being on the other side of the window. I could now see parts of his room that were once hidden from me... parts of his life. He had his letterman jacket draped over his bed frame, a poster for some 80s film I didn't recognise, and a shelf lined with miniature Lord of the Rings figurines. They looked like they'd been broken then haphazardly glued back together; and I remember what he'd said about his brother Jeremy messing with them. His chest of drawers was messy, socks hanging out from every direction and on top he had a lamp, small mirror, and a framed photo of his family. Finally, I took a proper look at Jeremy. He looked like just a regular kid, and they all looked so happy. It made me sad.

"I don't *want* to, but I suppose I should." I shrugged. I held my hands together on my lap, staring ahead, not wanting to make eye contact. As I did, I spotted the journal he had been writing in the first day he'd moved in. It was lying open on the desk with paper and pictures poking out just like Albert's, except it looked newer, obviously.

"Was it bad?" He asked and I shrugged again.

"It was... different to what I was expecting." I admitted. "For starters, I spent most of the time feeling guilty because I couldn't stop thinking about you, and I was supposed to be focussed on him." I said, honestly. "I guess I kind of knew the whole time that it couldn't work out... because someone else had taken his place."

Nate reached out his hand and held mine, stroking his thumb across my skin softly. His hands were so much bigger than mine.

"Then he turned out to be... well... not what he looked like in the pictures, I don't know, it was weird. He'd picked photos that kind of looked like him, but were definitely someone else, if that makes sense?" I explained before continuing. "His name wasn't Mason. His name was Tony and he wasn't eighteen like he said, he was 24." I admitted. "Which means he was 21 when he started talking to me... I was fourteen... and he was..." I stopped.

Nate put his arm around me and held me tight. I refused to shed another tear over that man. "Was that it then? Did you see him and leave?" Nate asked after a moment. I shook my head.

"He found the hotel we were staying at and came to see me. I mean, it wasn't hard to find, when I thought he was Mason I told him exactly where we were staying." I admitted. "We sat and... well, he tried to kiss me."

I turned to see Nate's reaction, and he looked sad. Did he feel sorry for me? I don't know. I kept talking. "I slapped him, called him a predator then ran back to the hotel room and blocked him on social media." I said and Nate looked like he was... smiling? "What?" I asked.

"I just can't picture you slapping a 24-year-old guy." He laughed and I hit him lightly in the arm.

"Hey! I'm hardcore when I want to be." I joked, and he grabbed me around the waist and pulled me up onto his lap almost effortlessly. I sat there, looking down at him with a small smile. This was definitely where I needed to be. I rested my forehead against his and looked him in the eyes. His gaze was soft, and his eyes were beautiful. "Can you promise me something?"

He nodded slowly.

"Please, don't lie to me, okay?" I asked. He didn't take his eyes off me. "If there's something going on, if there's a problem or you need to say something just... tell me."

He smiled and kissed me on the lips softly, stroking my cheek with his thumb as he held my neck. "I promise." He said against my lips. "As long as you promise me something in return..."

I looked at him, eyebrow raised as a smirk presented itself on his lips. "Okay..."

"Promise you'll let me call you little lady." He laughed and I shoved him, standing up and laughing, shaking my head.

He grabbed me and pulled me back down, and we laid

there together, looking in each other's eyes.

"Okay fine, I promise."

Epilogue

Nate and I ended up having an almost movie-like summer together. We spent countless hours at the reservoir, he took me on dinner dates and to the movies, we even babysat for his parents. When he was at work, I was either working with Tiffany, researching colleges, or going to therapy that Dad insisted on when he'd found out what actually happened with Tony.

"I think it's important you talk about what happened with a professional." He'd said a few nights after we'd got home from London. He and Mom had talked about the situation at length. Reluctantly, I'd agreed, mainly to get him off my case, but it ended up helping a lot.

June, my therapist, understands the temptations of talking to people online. She even told me she had some online friends herself. She explained that my experience with Tony was probably going to have an impact on future relationships, and it had.

For the first couple of weeks of our relationship, I was worried Nate was lying to me about every little thing, but I didn't worry him with that. He promised that he wouldn't lie, and I was going to trust him... still, therapy helped me let loose with all those feelings.

Mine and Nate's parents had put some money together and bought Nate a car to celebrate his final year of high school, and so he didn't have to drive the beat-up family car anymore. It was used, and had a few bumps and bruises, but I suppose we all did so who were we to judge. What I did know was that this meant Nate and I could come and go as we pleased, and that freedom was the best present ever.

Florence came to visit once more at the end of the summer. We'd spent an entire week together, and we'd started looking at New York apartments we could share next year when I move. Turns out, they're really fucking expensive.

Now, here we were, the first day of senior year.

"Nervous?" Nate said, reaching over and intertwining our fingers as he drove.

"Yep." I smiled. "You?"

"Yep." He repeated. We hadn't told anyone from school that we were dating. Well, no one except Daniella. She'd walked into my house one day and saw the two of us making out on the couch–since then she's always knocked.

I looked over at Nate and smiled. He was wearing his letterman jacket, which I told him was cheesy but there was no convincing him. I'd opted for a pair of shorts covered in sunflowers, a plain white t-shirt and one of my show hoodies that said 'CAST' on the back with my name. I'd made extra effort with my hair and make-up and had spent most of the drive staring at myself in the mirror. It's not every day you start senior year hand in hand with the school's quarterback and resident heart throb.

We drove into the parking lot and I noticed a group of jocks wearing their letterman jackets too. I guess it wasn't *that* cheesy.

"Ready?" Nate asked, parking the car then leaning over to kiss me quickly.

"As I'll ever be."

Acknowledgements

First, I want to thank you, whoever you are, for making your way to the end of my novel. That's something I never would have pictured happening in a million years! Thank you for supporting this book and Robin's story. I've adored every minute of writing it and I cannot tell you how grateful I am that you found it and read it yourself.

Next, I'd like to thank Elliot, who this book is dedicated to. He won't read it, I know that, he doesn't read much, but he's supported me through all my crazy ventures since the moment we became a couple and hasn't stopped for the seven years we've been together.

Now, my mum. She's always supported me writing and inspired me to continue. Who knows, maybe we'll get back to writing that book together one day.

I'd also like to thank my dad who, while growing up, made sure my grammar was top-notch. Always helps when one of your parents is a proof-reader.

A big thank you to Auntie Agg, one of my favorite people who helped me fall in love with books and reading.

Thank you to Vicky. You always believed in me, even in the times I didn't believe in myself. Your unwavering support has meant the world to me since we met. Some online friendships really are worth holding onto, and you are one of the greatest. You're my Florence.

To Jess, Fi, Lauren, India, Jill, Izzy and all the amazing musical theater folk I have in my life: thank you for inspiring me to continue with my passion.

To Rory, Katy, Parker, Steph, Clara, ZoZo, Madi, Ana, Bethan, Synn and every friend I've ever made online: I've been so lucky with the amazing people I've met over the years thanks to the internet and you've all changed my life. Also, thank you for letting me ask constant questions about what Americans are like and what you call things.

To my beta readers: Emily, Izzy, Shelley, Victoria, Dominic, Jess, Katy, Jasmine, Vicky and Charlotte – thank you for reading before it was perfected and helping me reach this point.

DID YOU ENJOY

WORLDS

AWAY FROM YOU?

LET US KNOW ON AMAZON BY LEAVING A REVIEW!

Printed in Great Britain
by Amazon

49387469R00222